You can't go home again…

"Where is Rogers?" Pickett asked, blinking in confusion at the individual who was most certainly *not* Julia's butler, whom he had inherited, along with all her worldly goods, when he'd married her. This man, though clad in the sober dark suit of the London butler, could give Rogers ten years or more, and had the wrinkles to prove it. Or perhaps the wrinkles creasing his forehead were merely part of the bewilderment writ large upon his face.

"Who, sir?"

"Rogers," echoed Pickett. "My butler."

"One would suppose, sir, that your butler would be at your house."

"But—but this *is* my house," Pickett insisted.

"I fear you are mistaken." The butler's nose twitched, and Pickett realized with some indignation that his breath was being tested for any trace of alcohol. "This house has been the Town residence of the Dowager Countess of Wakesworth for the last twelve months and more."

Nowhere Man

Another John Pickett Novella

Sheri Cobb South

NOWHERE MAN

1

Which Finds John Pickett Nursing a Secret

I suppose I'd best be getting back to work."

With this unenthusiastic pronouncement, John Pickett, formerly of Bow Street, set aside his tea cup and rose to his feet. He crossed the hall and reclaimed the knitted muffler he'd surrendered to the butler upon stopping in Curzon Street to partake of a light nuncheon with his wife and his ten-year-old half-brother. It was only mid-October, but already the wind was keen and the skies heavy, hinting at the coming winter.

Julia rose as readily as her pregnancy (now in its seventh month) would allow, leaving young Kit in sole possession of the tray of fairy cakes—a tray which would very likely be empty when she returned from accompanying her husband to the door. "Poor love! Are you not making much progress on this case, then?"

"What makes you say so?" he asked, a bit more sharply than the question warranted.

The faint note of defensiveness in his tone was enough to make her blink at him in surprise. "Why, only that you don't talk about it much."

"You have enough on your mind," he said with a vague gesture toward the drawing room and the pile of small linen shirts he'd interrupted her in the act of mending.

"On the contrary, I don't have nearly enough! If it weren't for Kit tearing through his clothes at an astounding pace, I should very likely be bored to distraction. In all seriousness, John, if there is anything I can do to help—"

"Thank you, sweetheart, but no." He summoned a feeble smile. "I'm afraid any investigation is nine parts tedium, really."

"In that case, I shall see you this evening," she said, accepting this dismissal with a good grace. "Cook is preparing veal cutlets, so don't be late."

"I shan't be—but it won't be veal cutlets that I'll be hurrying home for," he said, drawing her as close as the bulge of her abdomen would allow.

He kissed her lingeringly, then waited until she had closed the door behind him before setting out on foot for nowhere in particular. Much as he loved Julia—and he loved her very, very much indeed—it was something of a relief to leave her, and to drop the pretense of being busy working on an investigation. Of being busy doing anything, for that matter, ever since he had left Bow Street under a cloud of suspicion, even though Mr. Colquhoun, his magistrate—his *former* magistrate, rather—insisted there was no such thing.

It was funny, in a way. He'd never had any illusions about his good name.

Never, that is, until he'd been faced with the prospect of losing it.

When Mr. Colquhoun had suggested that he might take on private commissions for those persons of his wife's class who might balk at flinging open the family closets and subjecting their skeletons to Bow Street's inspection, he had not been optimistic, and yet it had seemed as good an idea as any other; after all, he could hardly support his aristocratic bride by returning to his old profession of hauling coal, and still less could he go back to picking pockets in Covent Garden. Unfortunately, the well-heeled, scandal-averse individuals who were to have provided his livelihood had failed to materialize.

And so, less than a year after he had chided Julia for withholding information from him during the Sir

Reginald Montague affair, he had deliberately lied to her. Granted, it had never been his intention to deceive her, but when she'd asked about his frequent absences from home, he had fobbed her off with so feeble an explanation that she had been quite certain he must be investigating a matter of great delicacy. Rather than disabuse her of this pleasant notion, he'd created such a case from whole cloth.

Worst of all, if he were forced to make the decision again, he was not at all certain he would not have done the same thing. She had seized upon Mr. Colquhoun's suggestion with such eagerness that he couldn't bear to disappoint her by telling her the scheme she'd embraced so eagerly was a failure.

No, not the scheme. It was not the magistrate's suggestion that had failed; it was he himself.

And he, coward that he was, could not bring himself to admit his failure to Julia. Not that she would utter a word of reproach. On the contrary, she would remain steadfastly loyal, would even make excuses for his lack of progress.

But he didn't want excuses, and he certainly didn't want her to feel compelled to offer them. No, he wanted *accomplishments*, the sort of accomplishments that would make her former friends and acquaintances admit that perhaps Lady Fieldhurst had not done so very badly in her second marriage after all. God knew her loyalty and her love deserved *some* reward—namely, a worthier object.

Unfortunately, it appeared she was unlikely to have it. He had toyed once before with the idea of releasing her from an unequal marriage by putting a period to his own existence, but he'd discovered he had not possessed the courage to put such a plan into action. Ironically, that same scheme would be the act of a coward now, given that he'd placed upon her shoulders the dual burdens of a child on the way and a ten-year-old boy.

Finding that his steps had led him to the piazza at Covent Garden, he leaned against one of the pillars supporting the portico of St. Paul's Church and looked out over the bustling fruit and vegetable market, recalling a time not so very long ago when he'd stood in this same spot, searching for a young woman who sold cabbages. That young woman was dead now, murdered by her felonious lover in retaliation for her leading Bow Street—in the form of Pickett himself—practically to their doorstep. Nor had she been the first woman to die in the course of his investigations, for there had been another only a few months earlier in the Lake District. Really, he thought, much struck, he seemed to have a singularly deleterious effect on the female of the species. Perhaps it was a good thing he'd left Bow Street, after all. No, he amended, following this line of reasoning to its inevitable conclusion, perhaps it would have been better if he'd never been born in the first place.

But it was too late for that—twenty-five years too late—and so, in the absence of any better option, it remained only for him to find some way of passing the time until he could return to Curzon Street without arousing his wife's suspicions. The first few days he had spent thus engaged, he had entertained hopes of stumbling upon some crime in progress—a remnant of his early days with the Bow Street Foot Patrol, no doubt—which he could take a hand in stopping, and for which he might perhaps earn some reward, preferably in the form of pounds sterling. As one uneventful day succeeded another, he'd lowered his sights from persons to pets: finding a lost dog, or else rescuing a cat who'd got itself stuck in a tree. Finally, his ambitions had become even more modest, to the point that he only wanted somewhere to loiter without attracting the notice of his former colleagues.

Gradually he became aware that one of the costermongers was trying to catch his eye—a short, plump woman with cheeks as round and rosy as the apples she offered for sale. He answered her gap-toothed grin with a rather forced smile, then pushed his shoulders away from the pillar and made his way to the place where she'd set up shop. He selected one of the apples, and paid the woman twice the price she asked—a recklessly extravagant gesture for a man out of work, to be sure, but an oft-repeated one, carried out in the vague hope that it might somehow atone for the theft of another apple fully a decade earlier. Alas, it never did. Instead, the gratitude expressed by the recipient only made Pickett feel worse, knowing that it was wholly undeserved.

And so it proved once again.

"God bless you, sir," the apple seller said warmly, squirreling the coins away in her bodice as if fearful he might change his mind and demand the return of one. "God bless you for your kind heart."

"It's nothing, really—" he demurred, but it appeared she wasn't finished yet.

"And you mustn't think such a thing. You're quite wrong, you know."

"It's only tuppence. I assure you, I can well afford it," he added with a humorless little laugh. It was true, for what it was worth. Money was not a problem, thanks to Julia's jointure from her first marriage. He had finally come to uneasy terms with the fact that he would never be able to provide for her as well as her first husband had done, but to bring nothing at all to the marriage, not even the pitiful twenty-five shillings a week that had constituted his Bow Street wages, was quite another matter, especially now that she was expected to feed, clothe, and educate his young half-brother in addition to their own child.

"Pshaw! I'm not talking about money! I'm talking about your not having been born."

"I—I beg your pardon?" He had indeed been indulging in just such a maudlin train of thought, but he was fairly certain he had not spoken the idea aloud, and certainly not at sufficient volume that it could have been discerned over the din of commerce, and at such a distance.

"It wouldn't have been better at all," she continued, carefully rearranging the apples on top of her basket in order to fill in the gap left by his purchase.

"I—I'm sorry—I don't quite—"

"Of course you do! I heard you. And I tell you, you're quite wrong."

"But—how—"

The question he struggled to frame was to remain unasked, however, for at that moment a disturbing sight drove the curious exchange from his mind.

Amidst the wagons and carts choking the street, a single horse picked its way through the pedestrians thronging about the open market, clip-clopping slowly but steadily in his direction—a horse whose rider wore the blue coat and red waistcoat of the Bow Street Horse

Patrol. The man's black hat was pulled down to offer its wearer protection against the sharp wind. Pickett, however, didn't have to see the fellow's face to recognize Harry Carson.

The prospect of being seen like this, alone and unemployed, by one whom he had once outranked in the Bow Street hierarchy, was intolerable. He stuffed the apple into his pocket, then drew himself up to his full height and strode purposefully away from the market.

Right into the path of a drayman's wagon.

Chaos ensued. A woman screamed and the drayman sawed at the reins, cursing fluently as he struggled to avoid running Pickett down while simultaneously maintaining control over his startled team. He might have eventually succeeded in this endeavor had the apple seller not felt it incumbent upon her to offer some assistance. She hurried into the fray, knocking over in her haste a tall basket of oranges offered for sale by a fellow costermonger, who had no intention of allowing such blatant contempt for her own wares to go unchallenged. As the ensuing quarrel escalated quickly from what is euphemistically called "exchanging pleasantries" to pulling first caps and then hair, the horses took exception to the orange globes rolling and bouncing underfoot.

Pickett, seeing that becoming embroiled in such a

mêlée was hardly the best way in which to avoid the notice of even so oblivious an investigator as Harry Carson, judged it time to beat a strategic retreat. He might have been successful in this endeavor, had he not stepped on one of the oranges so plaguing the horses. It rolled out from under him, taking his foot with it. Pickett grasped wildly for the nearest support, and succeeded only in pulling a tall basket of cabbages down upon himself as he fell. Then his head struck the pavement, and Pickett knew no more.

2

In Which John Pickett Receives a Shock

Get back, now, and give him some air! He's coming 'round."

Pickett recognized the voice, and groaned aloud. Somehow it seemed of a piece with all the rest, that the first voice he should hear, in the wake of an accident as humiliating as it was painful, would be Harry Carson's.

"Are you all right, old fellow?"

There was no trace of mockery in the question, and Pickett opened his eyes. He was stretched out full-length in the middle of the market, his throbbing head cushioned by the knitted muffler—a gift from Mrs. Colquhoun the previous Christmas—which someone had removed from about his neck in order to fold into a makeshift pillow. A circle of curious onlookers surrounded him, a circle that included the drayman, now looking somewhat abashed, and the woman with the basket of oranges; of her rival in the same profession, the apple seller who had so disconcerted him, there was no sign. Rather nearer at hand, his former colleague knelt beside him, regarding him with every appearance of concern in his blue eyes.

"I say, are you all right?" Carson asked again. "Is there anyone I should send for?"

"You're not to go worrying Julia with this, if that's what you're getting at," Pickett said firmly. At least, he'd intended to speak firmly; instead, his voice was shaky and weak.

"Julia?" Carson seized upon the name. "Your wife, perhaps?"

"Yes, my wife," Pickett said with some asperity as he cautiously raised himself to a sitting position. "You've met Julia—Mrs. Pickett—before."

"Your name is Pickett, then?"

"Cut line, Harry. You know full well—"

"You know who I am?" Carson sounded not only surprised, but gratified by the fact.

"Of course I know who you are! I assure you, there's nothing wrong with my memory—nothing wrong with me at all that rest and willow bark tea won't set to rights," he added, putting a hand to his throbbing head. "But I've known you for months. We investigated that business at Dunbury together."

At this reminder, Carson's look of surprised pleasure faded. "Er, maybe you'd better come with me. You can wait in comfort at the Bow Street Public Office while someone sends for your wife—Julia Pickett, you said?—to come and fetch you."

"*Bow Street?*" Pickett recoiled as if Carson had suggested they seek out a comfortable snake pit or lion's den. "No! I don't want—that is, I wouldn't like to impose on Mr. Colquhoun—"

"Believe me, Mr. Colquhoun won't be overly troubled," Carson drawled.

Under different circumstances, Pickett might have pressed him to explain this cryptic remark. But Carson's whole demeanor toward him was so odd that Pickett doubted that his explanation would be any more enlightening than the rest of his conversation had been.

"Thank you, Harry, but there's no need for you to go to any trouble. I'm perfectly capable of going home on my own."

In proof of this statement, he clambered to his feet and dusted himself off. The circle of spectators had begun to disperse, seeing the show was over, and so Pickett had no difficulty in walking past them, although he was not so steady on his pins as he would have liked.

A long walk in the brisk air went some way toward restoring him, and by the time he reached Curzon Street, Pickett felt much himself again. It was a great pity that he could not say the same for everyone else. As he approached the tall, narrow house where he lived with his wife, he saw a few of the neighbors out and about in spite of the autumnal chill in the air, although not so many as there would have been in months past, when the weather was warmer and the days longer. It was not the number of people that puzzled him, however, but their behavior. To be sure, the general attitude toward him had never been warm; his birth was too far beneath theirs to permit of approval, much less friendship. But on this occasion, they seemed not to notice him at all. Even the few with whom he exchanged nods returned the gesture not with the frigid civility he had come to expect, but with the distant courtesy one might accord a stranger. Shaking off a vague feeling of disquiet, he strode up the broad, shallow steps of number twenty-two, and opened the door.

Or he tried to. Finding it locked, he was obliged to resort to the brass knocker mounted in the middle of the door just below eye level. It opened a moment later, and Pickett found himself staring into the face of a total stranger.

"Where is Rogers?" he asked, blinking in confusion

at the individual who was most certainly *not* Julia's butler, whom he had inherited, along with all her worldly goods, when he'd married her. This man, though clad in the sober dark suit of the London butler, could give Rogers ten years or more, and had the wrinkles to prove it. Or perhaps the wrinkles creasing his forehead were merely part of the bewilderment writ large upon his face.

"Who, sir?"

"Rogers," echoed Pickett. "My butler."

"One would suppose, sir, that your butler would be at your house."

"But—but this *is* my house," Pickett insisted.

"I fear you are mistaken." The butler's nose twitched, and Pickett realized with some indignation that his breath was being tested for any trace of alcohol. "This house has been the Town residence of the Dowager Countess of Wakesworth for the last twelve months and more."

"But—but that's impossible! My wife bought this house not long after her husband died." Realizing the illogic of this claim, he added, "Her first husband, that is; not me, obviously."

The butler's expression conveyed the information that he saw nothing "obvious" about the situation, whatever Pickett might say to the contrary. To Pickett, there was only one possible explanation: Julia *knew*.

Somehow she had discovered the truth about his "investigation," and had settled on this method of punishing him for his deceit. He wasn't quite certain why, or what she hoped to achieve by it, but he had to admit she had done her work well. The butler's demeanor was perfect, while as for the house...

He glanced over the butler's shoulder to the marble-tiled hall and the drawing room just visible beyond it. How in the world had she managed to refurnish the house in the time since he'd left after nuncheon? Even the walls were a different color, although there was no smell of fresh paint. Had they been papered, perhaps? Still, to accomplish such a task and then remove every trace of it must have taken a considerable time—more time, surely, than had elapsed since he had taken his leave of his wife.

"Look here, can I just see Julia—er, Mrs. Pickett, that is?"

"I regret that I cannot oblige you, sir, but there is no one here by that name." The butler's tone was clearly calculated to inform the caller that he saw nothing amusing about a joke in very poor taste. In this, at least, Pickett found himself in complete agreement with the man.

"The mistress of the house, then," amended Pickett, rapidly losing his patience. "Whatever she chooses to call herself."

The butler gave him a reproachful look, but left to carry out this request. He returned a few minutes later with the information that "Her ladyship, the Dowager Countess of Wakesworth, will see you."

Upon being instructed to "follow me," Pickett was led into a salon which he knew as the drawing room. But instead of the sunny chamber where he'd made a habit of joining his wife for tea whenever his Bow Street investigations took him to Mayfair, he found himself in a room whose heavy crimson velvet curtains completely shut out the light, requiring the use of candles even in the middle of the day. Paintings in heavy gilt frames covered the walls, and Julia's delicate Hepplewhite furnishings had been replaced by the elaborately scrolled and gilded pieces of the previous century. But the most disturbing part of this rococo nightmare was the woman rising from the sofa to greet him—a gaunt, silver-haired lady with fully three quarters of a century in her dish, clad in the boned bodice and panniered skirts of her younger days.

"Good afternoon, Mr.—Pickett, was it?" She held out a gnarled hand upon which a large green stone glowed. "What may I do for you?"

"I—I'm looking for my wife," Pickett stammered, no longer so certain of his footing.

"And you have some reason to believe she might be here?"

"It's a long story," Pickett confessed with a sigh.

"I'm sorry I can't be of more assistance, but I've been here alone all day. What is your wife's name, pray?"

"Julia. Julia Pickett." Seeing no sign of recognition in the woman's expression, he added, "Before our marriage, she was Lady Fieldhurst."

Her reaction astounded him.

"In that case, I have nothing more to say to you." She reached for the bell pull and gave it an emphatic tug. "Good day, sir."

"Look here, I'm sure this has all been very amusing," said Pickett, who was sure of no such thing, "but I've had my fill of it."

"Then I suggest you drop this very ill-bred play-acting at once, and leave this house before I summon the constable."

The butler entered the room in answer to the summons. "You rang, your ladyship?"

"Indeed, I did. Pray show this man off the premises."

"Certainly, your ladyship. Come along, sir."

"But—what—Julia—I don't—"

He might have saved his breath. The butler was surprisingly strong in spite of his advanced years, and Pickett, unwilling to risk injuring the fellow by fighting back as he might have done against a younger man, found himself seized by the arm and frog-marched out of the room and through the front door.

"But—Julia—"

"If it's Lady Fieldhurst you're looking for, I suggest you begin with the newspapers," Lady Wakesworth called after him, but before he could ask her to explain this cryptic utterance, the butler closed the door in his face.

"But—but—what just happened here?" Pickett asked of no one in particular, staring at the door.

The door, unsurprisingly, offered no assistance, but a faint, metallic *click* gave Pickett to understand that the key had been turned in the lock, forestalling any further attempts at invading the premises.

Thus forced to concede defeat, he turned away and staggered down the steps and onto the pavement. He looked wildly from one end of the street to the other, searching for someone—anyone!—who might offer some idea as to where Julia had gone, but the street was almost deserted. The only sign of life was a short, stout woman pushing a wheeled cart—a common enough sight in Covent Garden, but a rare one in this genteel residential neighborhood.

"Hey! You there!" Pickett shouted as the hem of her dark skirt disappeared around the corner. Breaking into a run, he reached the corner and turned, half fearing to discover that she had disappeared without a trace. But no, there she stood, watching the street corner as if she were waiting for him.

"You were in Covent Garden less than an hour ago," he said, panting from exertion. "I bought an apple from you."

"And paid me very well for it, too," she agreed, nodding.

"What are you doing here?"

"Selling apples, of course." She picked up one, and turned it over for his inspection. "Would you like another?"

He shook his head impatiently. "No, that's not—I mean—you said—" He broke off, and tried again. "Something strange is happening here, and you seem to know something about it. About me, I mean."

"My dear boy, what could I possibly know about you? After all"—she gave him a wink—"you've never been born."

3

*In Which John Pickett Encounters
an Old Lover and a Dead Man*

Leaving Pickett to ponder the significance of this bizarre statement—if, in fact, it possessed any significance at all—she turned and walked away, and was soon swallowed up in the crowd.

"Wait! Come back!"

Pickett pushed his way through the pedestrians choking the pavement, to the annoyance of several, and once almost tripped over a beggar—a veteran, to judge by the ragged uniform jacket that offered his only protection against the cold—seated on the ground with his back against the wall and his one remaining leg stretched out before him. Pickett muttered a hasty apology and would have dropped a few coins into the man's tin cup, but when he reached into his pockets, he came up empty. He had not long to wonder at this curious circumstance, for his thoughts were all for the apple seller. She obviously knew something, and he fully intended to collar her and have the truth out of her. She couldn't have got far, not while trying to push a cart down a crowded street, and she could hardly have vanished into thin air.

It soon appeared, however, that that was exactly what she *had* done. Certainly there was no sign of her, although Pickett twice embarrassed himself by accosting short, plump women who, when they turned their bonneted heads to him, proved to be complete strangers.

Clearly, the woman, whoever she was, did not wish to be found. It was obvious, then, that he could look for no assistance from that source. Still, the fact remained that Julia was not in the Curzon Street house. Where, then, might she be? Pickett didn't know, but he bethought himself of someone who might: Emily, Lady Dunnington, whose husband held a seat in the House of Lords, and who must surely have returned to London for the autumn session. And where Lord Dunnington went, Pickett reasoned, Lady Dunnington and their infant daughter would undoubtedly follow; after years of estrangement, the recently reconciled couple appeared to be making up for lost time, if Lady Dunnington's letters to Julia were anything to judge by.

Now that he had a plan, Pickett lost no time in setting out for the Dunnington house in Park Lane. He would have sent up one of his cards, but these, too, had vanished from his coat pocket, and so he was obliged to convey his request by word of mouth. The butler nodded, and a moment later Pickett was ushered into the presence of not Lady Dunnington, but her lord and master, a dignified gentleman of about fifty—and one, moreover, whom Pickett was clearly interrupting just as he was prepared to go out.

"Mr. Pickett, is it?" Lord Dunnington asked, glancing rather pointedly at the long-case clock standing against the wall. "What may I do for you?"

"Your lordship." Pickett executed an impatient bow. "I'm sorry to impose on you, but I had hoped for a word with your lady."

The earl heaved a world-weary sigh. "I see. I daresay I can hazard a guess as to the nature of your business with her."

"I rather doubt it, my lord. I, er, I seem to have misplaced my wife, and wondered if Lady Dunnington might offer some assistance—"

" 'Assistance'? Is that what they're calling it these days?" asked Lord Dunnington with a bitter little laugh. "Well, it's original, I'll grant you that. I hate to be the bearer of bad news, but Lady Dunnington is not at home."

"Oh?" The claim was innocent enough on the face of it, but a prickling on the back of Pickett's neck signaled a warning nonetheless.

"In fact, Lady Dunnington has not been 'at home' in almost ten years," continued his lordship. "If you wish to discover her present whereabouts, you would do better to ask Sir Reginald Montague."

Pickett started at the familiar name. "But—but Sir Reginald Montague is dead!"

"Dead?" the earl echoed sharply. "Since when?"

"Almost a year ago." Seeing his lordship's memory was in need of prompting, Pickett added, "He was shot to death at close range."

Lord Dunnington shook his head. "A charming thought, I'll admit, but I fear you are misinformed. For the last year, Sir Reginald Montague has been in blooming health, as evidenced by the intimate con-nection he currently enjoys with my wife."

"But—the baby—" Pickett protested.

His lordship's eyebrows rose in an expression indicative of mild curiosity. "Is there to be a child, then? I suppose I shouldn't be surprised, under the circum-stances. I daresay I won't be the first man in London obliged to feed, clothe, and house another man's child.

Thank God my wife and I have the two boys, so I need have no fears of my family's heritage going to a cuckoo in the nest. Now"—he glanced at the clock again—"if you will excuse me, the Lords will be convening soon, and I must be present for the discussion on how best to respond to this business at Carlisle."

As one of his last cases with Bow Street had uncovered a plot by Irish sympathizers to seize Carlisle Castle, the mention of the town that shared its name caused Pickett's hackles to rise. "What business?" he asked, and this time there was no trace of a stammer.

"High treason, to begin with. As you may be aware, Carlisle Castle was seized by Irish rebels over the summer. The timing couldn't be worse. We must quash the revolt before the rebels can enlist France's aid— which they would be eager to give, as it would land Bonaparte on our very doorstep—but most of our forces are engaged on the Peninsula and can't be spared. Whatever Parliament decides, the casualties on both fronts are bound to be high." He took Pickett's elbow and steered him toward the door. "I regret that I could not be of more assistance, but if I hear any word of your wife— Mrs. Pickett, was it?—I will send word. I must caution you not to be optimistic, but if I should chance to learn anything to the purpose, where may I reach you?"

This was a matter Pickett had not considered.

Strangers were living in the house he shared with Julia, and his prospects of hiring lodgings for the night were dim, as his pockets were to let. He stammered something about not wanting to put Lord Dunnington to any trouble, and turned his attention to the task that had just become urgent.

He had to find Julia before nightfall.

* * *

Since Lady Dunnington's reconciliation with her husband had apparently been short-lived, Pickett lost no time in seeking her out in Audley Street, where she had maintained an independent establishment during their long estrangement.

"Yes, sir?" prompted Jack, the footman who answered the door.

Granted, the fellow did not seem to remember him, but this, Pickett told himself, was hardly surprising; it had been almost a year since Jack had fetched him from Bow Street to investigate the murder of Sir Reginald Montague, and the footman had been suffering from the ague at the time. In fact, he had been rousted from his sickbed only long enough to carry out his errand to Bow Street before Lady Dunnington had sent him back to bed with a drop of brandy laced with lemon—an unexpected kindness which had given Pickett to understand that her ladyship was not so callous as he had previously supposed. It was that unexpected tenderness of heart to which he was determined to appeal now.

"I should like to see Lady Dunnington, if you please," he told Jack.

"Begging your pardon, sir, but her ladyship is not receiving," was the unpromising reply.

"I understand, and I'm sorry to impose on her, but the matter is—is one of some urgency."

Pickett had never quite mastered the ability to conceal his emotions behind a mask of indifference, and if the footman had any doubts as to the truth of the caller's claim, he had only to look at Pickett's face to decide that the "matter," whatever it was, was indeed desperate.

"If you will excuse me, I will inform her ladyship," Jack said with all the eagerness of a man announcing his intention of having a tooth drawn. "Who may I say is calling?"

"John Pickett."

Jack departed with some trepidation, leaving Pickett to cool his heels in the front hall while his message was delivered. He had not long to wait before the sound of a door opening indicated that he was no longer alone. Shifting his gaze from its contemplation of the floor (which he'd been examining in vain for some trace of Sir Reginald Montague's bloodstains), he saw that the new arrival was not Lady Dunnington, as he had expected, but a woman standing in the doorway that led downstairs to the servants' domain, a doe-eyed young woman whose flaxen hair was imperfectly concealed by a starched mobcap.

"Oh!" she exclaimed in a startled voice. "I beg your pardon. I didn't realize—"

"*Dulcie?*" Pickett interrupted, stunned into forgetting his manners. "*Dulcie Monroe?*"

"Why, yes, sir." She smiled timidly up at him. "Should I know you? I'm afraid I can't quite place you."

"John Pickett. I—" Here, however, words failed him. How did one say *I thought you were in Newgate* without sounding demented, or boorish, or both?

Fortunately, he was spared the necessity of a reply by a voice that hailed him in somewhat impatient accents.

"Yes? What is it?"

Jack had clearly not lied when he'd said Lady Dunnington was not receiving. In fact, her ladyship was not even fully dressed, but was clad in a very fetching dressing-gown of frivolous and feminine design. Her dark hair was disheveled, either escaping from, or hastily put up with, its pins.

"I'm sorry to inconvenience you," Pickett began gamely, "but I'm looking for Julia."

"Julia—?" prompted her ladyship, clearly expecting some further enlightenment.

"Julia. Lady Fieldhurst." He wasn't quite sure why he hadn't said "Julia Pickett," except that the entire world seemed to have run mad, and in this world where nothing made any sense, the idea of his having married a viscountess—the only part that was actually true—somehow seemed maddest of all.

"Who wants to know?" Lady Dunnington asked warily. "You're not one of those men who writes gossip for the scandal-sheets, are you?"

"Good God, no!" Pickett answered impatiently. "Surely you must remember me—I'm John Pickett; I'm with—that is, I was with Bow Street."

Her ladyship gave a peal of laughter. "I wasn't aware that Bow Street was in the habit of engaging babes in arms."

This, at least, was Lady Dunnington as he remembered her. "I was called in to investigate Lord Fieldhurst's murder," he reminded her.

In an instant, her humor faded and her smile grew wintry. "That goes a long way toward explaining her present whereabouts."

As his wife's present whereabouts were exactly what he had come to discover, Pickett let the insult pass. Lady Dunnington remembered her friend's *mésalliance*, and for the moment, that was enough. It was with some relief that he said, "You know, then, that I married her."

"Married her what?" Lady Dunnington asked. "I should have thought her lady's maid was too old for you, besides being entirely too high in the instep."

"No, no!" Pickett insisted, realizing his relief had been premature. "She—Julia, I mean—Lady Fieldhurst —she married—"

"What the devil is taking so long, Emily? I haven't all day, you know," a new voice put in querulously, as a middle-aged gentleman with silver hair and cold blue eyes descended the staircase.

He was clad in a loose-fitting banyan of burgundy-colored silk, and the faint tuft of chest hair just visible at the top gave Pickett to understand that he wore nothing underneath. Pickett, left in no doubt as to exactly what he had interrupted, blushed crimson. He had never seen the man before—at least, he had never seen him alive— but he knew exactly who this was: Sir Reginald Montague, who had somehow survived being shot at close range a year ago in this very hall.

Pickett stammered an incoherent apology and stumbled back out into the street, no more the wiser than he'd been when he had first entered the house. As the door closed behind him (punctuated by a giggle from Lady Dunnington that suggested he and his unwelcome interruption had already been forgotten), he scanned the street for some sign of the apple seller, but saw none. If he couldn't find Julia soon, he reasoned, he would have to track the woman down, as she seemed to be the only person who might be able to tell him why everyone was acting so strangely, but his first priority was discovering what had happened to Julia, who had apparently been put out of her house by the old harpy now in residence there.

Fortunately, he was not entirely without resources. There was one more place he might try; in fact, it was quite possible that Julia, finding her presence at Lady Dunnington's house an imposition, had gone there already, and would be waiting for him at the Fieldhurst town house in Berkeley Square, presently occupied by the former George Bertram, cousin and heir presumptive of her first husband.

4

Which Has More Unpleasant Surprises
in Store for John Pickett

The days were growing shorter with the approach of winter, and long shadows fell across Berkeley Square by the time Pickett reached the Town residence of the current Lord Fieldhurst. He looked forward to the coming interview with the same eager anticipation which Lady Dunnington's footman had displayed at the prospect of interrupting her romantic tryst; still, if anyone would be aware of Julia's whereabouts, George, Lord Fieldhurst would be the man. He'd made it his business to keep up with her doings—and to express his disapproval of them—ever since the death of her first husband had made him, in the absence of direct heirs of the body, Viscount Fieldhurst and titular head of the

Bertram family.

Pickett lifted the brass door knocker and let it fall. A moment later, the door was opened by a stiff-rumped butler whose bulk effectively blocked the opening, denying any caller even a glimpse of the hall beyond.

"The family is not receiving visitors," he informed Pickett bluntly, and began to shut the door in his face.

"But I'm a member of the family," Pickett put in hastily, thrusting his foot into the rapidly narrowing gap to prevent the door from closing.

Clearly, the butler was not expecting this, and wasn't quite sure how to handle it. "I see," he said warily, giving Pickett an appraising look that made him glad he was wearing one of the new coats Julia had seen fit to bestow upon him; he suspected the butler would not have been impressed with his old brown serge. "If you will come in, sir, I will inform his lordship."

Pickett stepped inside, and the butler hastily closed the door behind him, as if fearful that all of London's great unwashed would attempt to sweep past him in Pickett's wake. Having successfully forestalled this calamity, he turned to address Pickett somewhat sheepishly.

"I meant no discourtesy, sir, but—well, under the circumstances, one can't be—but if you will give me your name, I will inform his lordship."

Pickett found himself reaching once again for a card case that wasn't there. In the absence of any written form of identification, he said, "Pickett. John Pickett."

"Very good, Mr. Pickett. I shall return directly." The butler left him standing in the hall and went up the stairs, presumably in search of his master. When he returned a short time later, his manner had undergone a change— and not for the better.

" 'Member of the family,' indeed! 'John Pickett'! His lordship says he has never heard of such a person in his life. Now, leave this house at once, before I summon the constable!"

George Bertram knows something, Pickett thought desperately. *He knows something, and he's not telling.* Granted, there had never been any love lost between him and George ever since Pickett, as a Bow Street Runner conducting his first investigation into a murder, had questioned the heir presumptive and uncovered a guilty secret of quite another sort. Still, George's sense of duty as head of his family had obliged him to recognize the second husband of his cousin by marriage, whatever his disapproval of the union. Now it appeared that grudging sense of obligation had its limits.

Pickett, undaunted, ignored the butler's threats and strode across the hall to the foot of the stairs.

"I know you're up there, George!" he shouted in the

general direction of the landing above. "Hide if you wish, but I'll find her, do you hear me? You may do your damnedest, but I will find her!"

Alas, Lord Fieldhurst's damnedest proved to be more than sufficient. Pickett's shouts had attracted the attention of most of the household staff, including two footmen—young men very nearly as tall as Pickett himself, and who outweighed him by three stone or more. The butler gave them a nod, whereupon they seized Pickett and bore him inexorably toward the door. They had not quite reached it when it flew open to admit a very young gentleman of about nineteen, clad in the exaggerated fashion of the aspiring dandy.

"I say, it's deuced cold out there. Daresay we might even have snow by morning," he complained, brushing at the fashionably peaked shoulders of his wasp-waisted tailcoat as if to rid them of any early snowflakes.

"Harold!" exclaimed Pickett. The last he'd heard of Harold Bertram, that young man had been a midshipman aboard His Majesty's frigate *Dauntless*. Pickett hadn't known the ship was in port, but he wasn't about to quibble at this stroke of good fortune. "I'm looking for Julia. Tell me—"

"Oh?" Harold asked in the bored drawl affected by the dandy set. "Julia who?"

"Your cousin Julia," Pickett said, impatient with the

young man's willful ignorance. He'd thought life in the Royal Navy had done much to improve Harold Bertram's character, but it appeared he'd been mistaken.

"If you mean who I think you mean, I must point out that she's no cousin of mine," Harold demurred hastily. "She's only the wife—widow, that is—of Papa's predecessor. Not a drop of Bertram blood in her veins, 'pon my soul."

"Harold, my pet, is that you?" called a fretful feminine voice, and to Pickett's utter astonishment, Caroline Bertram, George's bigamously wed second wife, hurried down the stairs. "Thank God you've come at last! I trust none of those dreadful newspaper persons accosted you. Your brothers are already here, and your father is determined that we shall none of us leave the house until this dreadful business is behind us, and the scandal has died down."

"Yes, I'm here, Mummy," said Harold, stating the obvious. "But I might have made the journey from Oxford hours ago if only Papa would stand the nonsense for a curricle and pair—which he can well afford, now that he's stepped into Cousin Frederick's shoes."

Caroline Bertram embraced her firstborn, and received from him a dutiful kiss on the cheek. "Now, Harold, you cannot have thought! A fine thing it would look, you tooling about Town in such a showy rig with *this* hanging over our heads! Really, it puts me all out of patience with Julia! Not that we haven't benefitted handsomely from it in some ways, of course, but I should have thought she would have more consideration for the family!" Having delivered herself of this complaint, she turned toward Pickett, still struggling to free himself from his captors. "Good heavens, is that fellow still here? Pray, get rid of him at once!"

Recalled to their duty, the beefy footmen lost no more time in thrusting Pickett bodily into the street and slamming the door shut behind him.

What the devil—? thought Pickett, picking himself up and dusting himself off. George and Caroline Bertram had never been legally wed. The lady who should have been living here—and who would no doubt have been far more sympathetic toward his quest—was George's first wife, married in secret when they were both very young. The scandal which had followed that revelation had been sufficient to drive poor Harold from Oxford. But apparently Harold was still there, or else had resumed his studies after only a very short stint in the navy.

It made no sense. None of it made any sense, and the only person who might be able to explain it all—the Covent Garden costermonger—had seemingly vanished off the face of the earth; certainly he could see no sign of her in the twilight that had by this time descended upon the elegantly manicured square.

Not that he would expect to see such a person in Mayfair, amongst England's aristocracy; her domain would be the fruit and vegetable markets where he had first seen her. Granted, there was her unexpected appearance in Curzon Street, but this was surely an aberration.

He stepped aside to make way for the lamplighter, realizing that with the darkness would come the farmers' wagons which, having traveled all day from the surrounding countryside, would be unloading their produce to be offered for sale the next morning. Wherever she might have been earlier in the day, the woman would surely have returned there to fill her cart with fresh wares for the following day. He would return to Covent Garden and find her, and this time he would not let her escape until he had some answers.

* * *

It was fully dark by the time he reached Covent Garden, for his progress had been slow. Clouds obscured the moon, and the streets were illuminated only by flickering circles of yellow light from the lamps that stood sentinel at regular intervals along the pavement. Still, the piazza bustled with activity in spite of the limited visibility. Wooden crates and coarse burlap sacks of potatoes, cabbages, and late beans were passed from hand to hand from the men on the wagons to their fellows on the ground, while beyond them, a bevy of women swarmed about the offloaded produce, selecting some samples and rejecting others as they filled their baskets in preparation for the next morning's commerce.

And among their number was a short, plump woman in a poke-fronted bonnet and a knitted shawl with a border of fringe.

Pickett could not quite bring himself to manhandle any female, regardless of the circumstances; still, his hand fell heavily upon her shoulder, and he gripped it firmly enough to forestall any attempt at escape.

Not that she appeared to be making any attempt to do so. In fact, she turned to regard him with every indication of pleasure, as if she had been hoping for just such a meeting.

"Why, good evening, dear boy! I hope you have spent a productive afternoon."

Pickett refused to be diverted. "A word with you, if you please."

"Of course! What may I do for you?"

Without releasing his grip on her shoulder, Pickett steered her out of the crowd to the portico of St. Paul's Church, where they might speak in relative privacy. "You may tell me just what the devil is happening! A stranger has taken up residence in my house, and I've just seen a man, alive and well, who was shot at close range following a dinner party hosted by a friend of my wife."

"It's as I said before," she explained with exaggerated patience. "You were never born. Sir Reginald Montague was never shot, because the dinner party never took place."

"You're saying Lady Dunnington wouldn't have hosted her dinner party if I had never been born? That makes no sense at all! Besides, what about the stranger living in my house? What about my wife? *Where is my wife?*"

And that was the matter in a nutshell, never mind Sir Reginald, or Dulcie, or even the lady now living in his house. He knew what it was like to be alone in London, having been turned out onto the streets to fend for himself at the age of fourteen. It was intolerable to think of Julia in such a situation. His background, at least, had given him some idea of how to survive on the streets, scavenging for food and sleeping in doorways or under bridges; presumably, his young half-brother would have similar resources to sustain him, at least until Pickett could locate him. Julia, on the other hand... Nothing in his gently-bred bride's experience would have prepared her for such an existence. A hundred things might happen to her—might already have happened, each scenario more terrible to contemplate than the one before.

"Where is my wife?" he asked again, pleadingly this time.

She gave him a rather pitying smile. "Look inside yourself, dear boy. You already know, don't you?"

Pickett threw out his arms in a gesture of helpless frustration. "How can I possibly know? How can I know anything at all, when nothing makes sense anymore?" A sudden thought occurred to him. "You said I had never been born, and yet here I am. What about Julia? Has *she* been born?"

"Oh, yes," she said, nodding reassuringly.

"If you won't tell me where she is, will you at least tell me—is she—is she safe?"

It seemed to Pickett that the woman hesitated a moment before saying, "She is in no immediate danger. But I'm afraid I won't be able to say the same for you, roaming the streets after dark, and you all alone. Get some sleep, dear boy, and perhaps in the morning you'll find the answers you seek."

Whatever he might have said to this advice was interrupted by an altercation between a draft horse and a stray dog in search of scraps. Pickett was not aware of having released his grasp on the woman's shoulder, but when he turned away from the fracas to ask her how he was to "get some sleep" when he hadn't so much as a roof over his head, the woman was gone, and the hand that had gripped her shoulder now hung over empty air.

5

In Which John Pickett Discovers
You Can't Go Home Again

Since there was clearly no more help to be had from that quarter, Pickett was left with the challenge of exactly where he was to sleep when his house was inhabited by strangers and he possessed not so much as a farthing with which to hire a room for the night. Aside from his wife and his half-brother, he had no other family beyond a father in Botany Bay and a nominal "stepmother" who had driven him from the house the very same day his father was transported. It was unlikely that any assistance would be forthcoming from so dubious a source, even if he could swallow his pride enough to ask for it.

In the absence of any blood relations, what other

connections might he have to whom he could apply for help? The obvious choice was, of course, his magistrate —his *former* magistrate—Mr. Colquhoun. And yet something Harry Carson had said made him reluctant to seek out this usually reliable source—afraid, perhaps, of what he might discover. Failing Mr. Colquhoun, his former landlady, Mrs. Catchpole, might extend him sufficient credit as to allow him the use of the flat above her shop, just for the one night. Provided it was unoccupied, of course, which was by no means a given.

There was only one way to find out. He set out for Drury Lane, and soon came to the chandler's shop whose upper story housed the small furnished flat that had been his home for five years. The shop, he knew, would be closed at this hour, so he knocked on the door with sufficient force that Mrs. Catchpole would be able to hear him from her own lodgings in the rear of the building. No one answered. He knocked again, rattling the latch this time for good measure. Still no answer.

Exceedingly loth to give up his best hope of shelter, he groped above the door frame for the key that used to be hidden there. Mrs. Catchpole had never approved of the irregular hours his investigations had often required, but she had reluctantly made this small concession, admitting that it was better than being awakened in the middle of the night to open the door to her boarder.

There was no key. He groped once again up and down the length of the door frame, then switched hands —as if that would make a difference!—and tried again. No key was hidden there. She must have ended the practice after he had married and moved out of the flat to take up residence in Julia's house.

"Mrs. Catchpole?" he called, hammering on the door with his fist. It was too early for her to be in bed, but he had no doubt he was interrupting her dinner. He only hoped she would hear him over the rattle of pots and pans. His stomach rumbled at the reminder that he'd had nothing to eat since nuncheon with Julia, and wondered wistfully if his former landlady might invite him to share her own repast. "Mrs. Catchpole, it's me—John Pickett."

From somewhere inside came the sound of heavy footsteps—Mrs. Catchpole hurrying to greet him, just as he'd anticipated.

Unfortunately, he had failed to predict the broom she clutched in her hands, swinging it to and fro like a weapon.

"Out! *Out!*" she commanded, as her broom made contact with his shoulder. "Shop's closed. You want anything, you'll have to wait 'til morning."

"I don't—*ow!*—I don't want to buy anything," Pickett protested, dodging the broom as it sailed past his head on its return trip, scattering straw in its wake. "I just need a place to stay for the night, and I wondered if—"

"Do I look like I'm running an inn? You want lodging, you'll have to—"

"Mrs. Catchpole, it's me," he said again. "John Pickett." He grabbed the end of the broom on its next pass, putting an end to the attack and forcing his former landlady to look at him, *really* look at him, for the first time since she'd opened the door. "Don't you remember me? I used to live in the flat upstairs." Although he had been very careful to keep his name out of the events that had followed his vacating the flat, he decided that, at the moment, he could use any bit of leverage he could get. And so he added, "I'm the one who discovered the cache of coins under the floor."

This, it appeared, had the desired effect. Her grip on the broom relaxed, and if Pickett had not been holding the business end, it would no doubt have fallen to the floor. "That was you, was it?"

"Yes!" Pickett cried with a sense of relief bordering on euphoria. "That was me! Surely new clothes and a haircut haven't changed me as much as all that!"

To his utter astonishment, Mrs. Catchpole snatched the broom out of his grasp and set to with a will. "Have you no shame?"—*Whack!*—"That you could leave in the middle of the night with two months' rent in arrears—" *Whack!*

"*What?* I never—"

"—And here you show up all tricked out in your fine new clothes, when there's my floor upstairs all torn out"—*Whack!*—"and Lord Lessing what owns this building demanding that I pay for the repairs from my own pocket—" *Whack!*

Pickett flung up one arm in a futile attempt to stave off the attack long enough to make the woman see reason. "Mrs. Catchpole, that wasn't—I wouldn't—"

"—Besides giving him back a buried treasure that I don't have and never did"—*Whack!*—"and saying he'll see me ruined if I don't hand it over—"

Pickett, deciding discretion was indeed the better part of valor, abandoned all attempts at self-defense, and took to his heels. He fled the shop with his irate landlady and her broom in hot pursuit. Once outside, he collapsed against the door while he contemplated this fresh disaster. Mrs. Catchpole, ruined? Why, she was the canniest businesswoman he'd ever known, deriving a modest but steady living for more than twenty years after the death of her husband had forced her to run the shop on her own. What had happened here? He had been obliged to return the treasure to Lord Lessing—although it had gone sorely against the grain with him to do so, it had belonged to the man by law—but not before coercing his lordship into granting Mrs. Catchpole the use of the property rent-free for the rest of her life. It seemed Lord Lessing had gone back on his word.

But no, Pickett recalled, his thinking growing clearer as his heavy breathing returned to normal, she had said the floor of the upstairs flat was completely ripped out. He had taken up only the one board, and he'd put it back in place after removing the cache of silver that had been concealed in the cavity beneath. If, as the apple woman claimed, he had never been born, then it appeared someone else had discovered the treasure—someone who had been so hopeful of discovering more that he'd all but destroyed the flat in the process. And then what? The fellow had decamped, apparently, in the middle of the night, saying nothing to Mrs. Catchpole of his discovery nor even paying the rent he owed…

If she thought him capable of such a betrayal, it was no wonder she'd beaten him about the head with a broom. He'd be tempted to beat such a fellow himself.

One thing was certain: He could not look to Mrs. Catchpole for lodgings, even if the flat were still habitable. Where else, then, might he turn? He cast his mind back still further, to the days before he had taken up residence under Mrs. Catchpole's roof. He'd spent five years working for a coal merchant, and although the work was grueling and dirty, it had come with a tiny bedchamber in the basement of Mr. Granger's house and a place at his servants' board. Pickett had seen Elias Granger only once in the years since then, but his old employer had seemed pleased at his visit. Granted, there was quite a difference between giving a former apprentice tea and agreeing to house him for the night; still, the hour was growing late, and Pickett's options were shrinking. And so he turned his steps toward Cecil Street and, upon reaching the collier's house, knocked wearily on the door.

As soon as the butler opened it, Pickett knew something was wrong, although he could not have said *how* he knew. To be sure, his first impression was one of prosperity: The interior of the house smelled of sawdust and fresh paint, and beyond the foyer, he could see glimpses of paint-spattered sheets swathing the drawing room furnishings. Nearer at hand, the crystal prisms of what appeared to be a large chandelier lay in a sparkling heap on the floor, partially protected by the tall wooden stepladder which had been positioned over it, and which would, presumably, soon be employed by the builder who would affix it to the ceiling. It appeared that some sort of improvements to the house were being made, but this, surely must be a good thing—mustn't it?

"Yes, sir?" prompted the butler, awaiting some indication as to the reason for the visitor's presence. The man did not seem to recognize him, but Pickett decided to let this slight pass; Mr. Granger's servants had been singularly unimpressed with the young thief whom their employer had taken on as a favor to an old friend, so it was quite possible that the butler was feigning ignorance out of spite.

"Oh, er, I beg your pardon. I should like to see Mr. Granger, if it isn't too late." As he recalled, the coal merchant still kept the early hours he had established in his younger days, when he had first begun to amass his fortune.

"I'm afraid it is, sir. About seven years too late, in fact."

"Oh?" Pickett asked warily, feeling once again the now-familiar prickling at the back of his neck.

"Mr. Granger died seven years ago."

"But—but that's impossible! I don't believe it!" In fact, Pickett had good reason for his skepticism, having seen and spoken to the supposedly deceased Mr. Granger a scant six months earlier.

The butler shrugged. "You may believe or not, it's nothing to me. Your disbelief won't make it any less true, however." Finding the caller at a loss, the butler took pity on him. "Mrs. Lumpkin is here, if you should wish to see her instead."

"Mrs.—Lumpkin, you say?" echoed Pickett, taken aback by the introduction into the conversation of a name he'd never heard in his life.

"Mr. Granger's married daughter. Miss Sophy, as was."

"Sophy—you mean Lady Gerald Broadbridge, surely?"

The butler's brow puckered. "I'm not quite sure how you should know about that—not many people do, outside the families themselves. It's true that there was once some talk of a match between Miss Sophy and Lord Gerald, but all that came to an end when it was discovered that"—his voice lowered to a discreet whisper—"that Miss Sophy was in the family way."

"Oh?" Pickett, under no illusion as to the "honor" upon which the upper classes placed so much emphasis, thought the younger son of a duke would have no scruples about debauching a not-entirely-innocent daughter of the rising industrial class, much less one who had no doubt been an eager participant in her own debauchment. Still, he would not have thought Lord Gerald would let Sophy's dowry slip through his hands so easily. "And having had his way with her, Lord Gerald drew back from the betrothal?"

"There's the thing." By this time, the butler had apparently determined that Pickett, in spite of his ignorance of its patriarch's passing, was sufficiently intimate with the family that he might speak freely. "It wasn't Lord Gerald who had, er, done the deed. That honor, it seems, belonged to the footman."

"I see," Pickett said, remembering the many times Sophy had kept his own youthful ardor in line by threatening to favor the footman with her attentions. It seemed she had made good on the threat. Unless… "Tell me," Pickett began thoughtfully, "do you recall an apprentice who came to live here? It would have been about ten years ago. His name was John." His voice shook a bit on the final word. It felt strange to speak of himself as if he were someone else. It felt stranger still to speak of himself as if he no longer existed. Or, perhaps, as if he never had.

"I'm afraid you must be mistaken," the butler said, shaking his head. "Mr. Granger would never have allowed an apprentice to live under his own roof, for fear the lad might have designs on Miss Sophy."

"He did," Pickett muttered under his breath. "Poor fool."

The butler's brow puckered. "I beg your pardon?"

"Never mind. But—Mrs. Lumpkin, you said?"

"Yes, for she married the footman. Quite a step down from Lord Gerald Broadbridge, but what else was poor Mr. Granger to do but insist the blackguard make an honest woman of her? The shame of it killed him, though. The doctor called it a heart attack. A broken heart, more like." He shot a disapproving glance over his shoulder at the detritus of the construction trade. "And perhaps it's just as well he didn't live to see Miss Sophy and young Dick—I beg your pardon, I should say Mr. Lumpkin, seeing as he's now the master—as I say, the pair of them letting the fortune poor Mr. Granger amassed by the sweat of his brow run through their hands like water, and neither of them having any more thought for the business than their boy has, for all he's only six years old."

Pickett made a sympathetic noise that was not entirely feigned, and the butler was recalled to his duty. "But I mustn't keep you standing here. Did you want to see Mrs. Lumpkin, sir?"

Did he want to see Sophy? Granted, he had not enjoyed his last encounter with her, but while on that occasion she had been not at all pleased to discover that he had not worn the willow for her all these years, but had married another (and married a viscountess, at that), it was quite possible that this time she would not recognize him; after all, no one else had. One could hardly beg a room for the night from a seeming stranger—and the possibility that Sophy would be resolved not to remain strangers for long did nothing to reconcile him to the prospect.

"No, thank you," he told the butler. "I won't trouble

Miss Granger—that is, Mrs. Lumpkin. Good night."

With this avenue closed, there was only one thing he could do. He would find Mr. Colquhoun, and even if the magistrate did not remember him, well, Mr. Colquhoun's kindness would not allow him to cast a man in need out into the street. *At least, not the Mr. Colquhoun I know*, Pickett told himself as he set out in search of the magistrate, more than half afraid of what he would find.

The hour was late enough that the magistrate should have long since left the Bow Street Public Office, but as Pickett's present location was nearer to Bow Street than it was to Mr. Colquhoun's residence in Mayfair, he decided to stop there first, just in case the magistrate had stayed late.

But as he reached Russel Street, it seemed to Pickett that something was out of place—or, more accurately, that something was back *in* place, something that had, at least in the London he knew, been absent for almost a year.

Distracted momentarily from his search for Mr. Colquhoun, Pickett followed Russel Street to its intersection with Brydges Street, and his misgivings were confirmed: There on the corner stood the massive edifice that was Drury Lane Theatre. Evidently no performance was taking place that night, for the enormous building stood silent and tranquil in the darkness.

There was only one thing about the peaceful scene to give him pause.

The Theatre Royal at Drury Lane had burned to the ground eight months ago.

6

*In Which John Pickett
Is Reunited with His Magistrate*

On second thought, Pickett amended as he walked slowly toward the building that shouldn't have been there, not just one, but two things were wrong. For as he approached the theatre, he could see a printed placard in the circle of yellow light cast by a lamp on the street corner, a placard affixed to the front of the building announcing the appearance of Mrs. Elizabeth Church in the current production of Shakespeare's *Twelfth Night*, which would run until 15 January.

The last time he had seen Elizabeth Church—more familiarly known as Elspeth Kirkbride—she had abandoned the stage and was planning her wedding. Betrothals, he knew, might be broken, but how could one explain the sudden resurrection of a building that had burned to the ground—a building that, when he had last seen it only a few days ago, had just begun the long, slow process of rising from its own ashes?

Dismissing this new puzzle, at least for the moment, he hurried away in the direction of Bow Street. Whatever the changes that Harry Carson had hinted at, he would ask Mr. Colquhoun to put him up for the night; perhaps when he awoke in the morning, he would be able to make some sense of the strange new world in which he found himself.

Better yet, perhaps when he awoke in the morning, he would find himself in his own bed back in Curzon Street with Julia lying beside him, regarding him with a puzzled expression and wanting to know what in the world he had been dreaming, that had caused him to mutter and moan in his sleep all night long.

Having by this time reached the Bow Street Public Office, he entered the familiar building and looked about him. Besides the usual assortment of petty criminals and prostitutes, there were a few members of the Night Patrol, as well as a couple of his former colleagues, those principal officers colloquially known as Runners. Mr. Dixon was just putting on his greatcoat, and Mr. Griffin was in conversation with a constable who had brought in a juvenile miscreant, whom he now held by the collar of the boy's threadbare coat. Both men looked up briefly at his entrance before returning their attention to their previous activities. Either they had not forgiven him for his rôle in that business with the Bank of England, or else they did not recognize him at all. Pickett wasn't sure which prospect he found the most disturbing.

"Excuse me, Mr. Dixon," he said, approaching the senior Runner, "is Mr. Colquhoun still here?"

The older man's eyes narrowed. "Who wants to know?"

"John Pickett," he said impatiently. "Surely you must remember me. I used to—"

He broke off abruptly. The door to Mr. Colquhoun's office had just opened, and a third Runner emerged from the small chamber—a man in his mid-thirties, with straw-colored hair and a beak-like nose.

"Foote?" Pickett asked incredulously. "William Foote?"

"Aye." Cold blue eyes flicked over Pickett without recognition before turning to Dixon.

It appeared he could expect no help from his former colleagues. Not that Foote had any right to hold a grudge against any other Runner, Pickett thought in growing indignation; after all, Foote was supposed to be dead, having been shot by Mr. Colquhoun after burning down Drury Lane Theatre in an attempt to murder Pickett himself.

"No luck," Foote told Dixon, shaking his head. "He's determined to go."

Dixon muttered a curse under his breath. "I don't like turning him out into the street like this. I'd go with him, if I knew where he lived. Would he tell me, do you think?"

"He might," Foote conceded with a shrug. "Whether you could make any sense of it is another matter."

"You're talking about Mr. Colquhoun?" Pickett asked urgently. Receiving an answer in the affirmative, he pressed for more. "Is he ill?"

Foote gave a short bark of laughter. "You could put it that way. Not the word I'd choose, myself."

Ignoring this rider, Pickett strode to the door of the magistrate's office and stepped inside. "Mr. Colquhoun? Are you all right, sir? *Sir!*"

Mr. Colquhoun was standing at the coat tree, swaying on his feet as he struggled to untangle a knitted muffler from one of its hooks, but he turned at the sound of his own name, and Pickett's heart stood still in his chest. The magistrate's thick white hair stuck out from his head in all directions, as if he had just that moment been awakened from sleep. His eyelids drooped over bloodshot blue eyes, and his nose was swollen and red, laced with a latticework of broken blood vessels. In short, Mr. Colquhoun was drunk, and by all appearances his condition was not an infrequent one.

Pickett was well aware that the magistrate liked his whisky as much as any other Scotsman, but he had never known Mr. Colquhoun to drink to excess, and certainly not while he sat at the bench. As he watched in stunned disbelief, Mr. Colquhoun turned back to his struggle with the muffler.

"Damned thing—won't—" muttered the magistrate, punctuating the last word with a mighty tug that would have upset his balance and pulled the coat tree down on top of him, had Pickett not intervened.

"Here, sir, let me help." He steadied Mr. Colquhoun with one hand and the coat tree with the other and, once neither was in imminent danger of collapse, began disentangling the muffler from its hook. "Are you ready to go home, then? I'm heading that way myself. Why don't I accompany you?"

Actually, Pickett wasn't heading anywhere, at least not that he could tell. Still, he could hardly leave Mr. Colquhoun to make his own way home in his present condition, not when the man had stood as a surrogate father to him for the last ten years and more. He draped the muffler about the magistrate's neck, then removed the greatcoat from its hook and held it open.

"Much obliged t'you." Mr. Colquhoun peered over

his shoulder at the young man helping him on with his coat. "Who are you?"

Somehow those three little words hurt more than anything else he had experienced thus far today. "I'm—I'm no one in particular," Pickett said with perfect truth. "Just—a friend."

Having succeeded in easing the magistrate's arms into his coat sleeves (or, rather, easing the coat sleeves over the magistrate's arms, as Mr. Colquhoun displayed a tendency to miss his target), Pickett buttoned him up and set his hat firmly on his head. After assuring himself that the magistrate would not topple over without his support, Pickett stepped over to the desk and pinched out the flame of the candle that burned there, then took Mr. Colquhoun's arm and, after some difficulty, maneuvered him out the door.

"I'll take him home," he told Dixon and Foote, steering the magistrate past them. "I know where he lives."

"Who are you?" Dixon asked, frowning slightly.

"An old friend." Pickett didn't even try to remind them of the years he'd spent at Bow Street, first as a member of the Foot Patrol and then as a Runner. What would be the point? "I'll see that he gets safely home."

One of us might as well, he thought bleakly as they left the warmth of the Bow Street Public Office for the cold, dark street.

"Shall I summon a hackney for you, sir?" Pickett offered as they reached Long Acre, looking westward in the hopes of spying just such a vehicle. Alas, he found none, nor was the short segment of Long Acre from Bow Street to Drury Lane any more promising. Fortunately, Mr. Colquhoun did not seem to mind.

"Always walk," he declared, and the fisted hand that smote his chest gave Pickett to understand that this was the magistrate's boast regarding himself, rather than a command to Pickett. " 's good for the con-sti-tu-tion," he added, pronouncing the final word with painstaking precision.

"It is," Pickett agreed, although privately he felt he'd had quite enough of walking for one day, having crisscrossed London on foot three times already. "Perhaps the night air will, er, clear your head a bit, too," he added diplomatically.

Unfortunately, Pickett saw no sign of this hoped-for event. Twice he was obliged to steer the magistrate in the right direction when he would have taken a wrong turn, and once he only just succeeded in holding his mentor back when he would have stepped out in front of a closed carriage drawn by high-spirited bays. At one point Mr. Colquhoun began to sing a tune in Gaelic, even seeming disappointed when Pickett neglected to join him in this musical endeavor.

"You're not singing," he chided, giving Pickett a rather bloodshot version of the fierce scowl he knew from long experience.

"Er, no, sir," Pickett said apologetically. "I'm afraid I don't know the language."

"Damned *Sassenach*," grumbled Mr. Colquhoun, and took up his song again.

A lump formed in Pickett's throat. It wasn't the first time Mr. Colquhoun had referred to him by the term, and he knew it was no compliment. Still, it had become something of a term of affection in Mr. Colquhoun's mouth, at least when he, Pickett, was its target. This time, though, it had no meaning beyond the obvious: a Scotsman's expression of disdain for anyone of English extraction.

At last they reached the house and stepped up onto the portico, albeit not without difficulty, as Mr. Colquhoun's foot kept missing the low tread. Pickett knocked on the door, and a moment later it flew open to reveal not the butler, but Mrs. Janet Colquhoun, the magistrate's wife.

"*There* you are, Patrick! I've been so worried!" She slipped her shoulder beneath her husband's arm, shifting the burden of his weight from Pickett to herself with the air of one who had performed the operation many times before; clearly, this was not the first time he had come home in such a condition. "And it so bitter cold tonight, too! Come inside, and we'll get you warmed up before the fire."

The prospect of warming oneself before a fire sounded to Pickett like heaven itself. Alas, any hope he might have entertained that he was included in this invitation was dashed when her attention shifted from her husband to his rescuer. "Thank you for bringing him home. I'm that grateful to you. He's—he's always worse this time of year."

"It was no trouble at all," Pickett assured her, and if this was not entirely true, then it was a lie uttered with the best of intentions. "I'm glad to be able to help him, after all he's done for—but you say he's worse this time of year? Why? If you'll forgive me for asking," he added hastily.

"It's our son," she said, lowering her voice as if this could prevent her husband from hearing. And so it might, Pickett conceded, for the magistrate had begun singing again.

"That would be James," Pickett recalled, thinking of the man several years older than himself whom he had met the previous Christmas.

She shook her head. "No, I meant our second son, Adam. He was the most like his father of all our children.

But Adam died while he was still a wee lad, and my poor husband never recovered from the loss."

"I'm sorry," Pickett said, remembering the large and lively family with whom he had spent the previous Christmas. He hadn't realized they had also known their share of heartache.

"It's many years ago now, but at certain times of the year—the lad's birthday, and the anniversary of the day he died—my husband seeks consolation in drink. But he's a good man for all that, and I hope you'll not think the worse of him for his weakness, Mr.—?"

"Pickett. John Pickett." He was no longer surprised by the fact that once again someone who should have known him apparently did not.

Mrs. Colquhoun sighed. "I've often thought it was a pity we never had another child after that. Not that it would have replaced our Adam—I'm sure nothing could do that—but another son might have given his thoughts a happier direction. I'd hoped it would get better with the passing of time, but it's actually grown worse. He didn't begin drinking so heavily until our children were grown up and on their own, and the house was so empty and quiet."

Pickett hardly heard the end of this speech, for he was still considering the implications of its beginning. *Another son*, she'd said... Sadly, her grieving husband had fathered no more sons of his own. And yet, incredibly, Mr. Colquhoun—the Mr. Colquhoun Pickett remembered—had found an object for his frustrated paternal instincts in a skinny street urchin with a black eye and a broken nose.

"But I must not keep you, for you'll be wanting to seek your own bed on such a cold night as this," Mrs. Colquhoun said, turning her husband toward the stairs with the ease of long practice. "Thank you again for bringing him home, and may God bless you for your kindness."

"Mrs. Colquhoun, may I—" The words came out in a rush before Pickett regained control of his tongue. He could not beg her to house him for the night when she believed him to be a stranger, especially not when she had all she could handle just keeping her husband upright. "May I help you get him up the stairs?"

She turned back just long enough to shake her head. "That's very kind of you, Mr. Pickett, but I'll not inconvenience you any further. Thank you again, and good night."

And with that, Pickett was gently but firmly dismissed.

7

*In Which John Pickett
Returns to the Old Neighborhood*

At least he could be certain that Mr. Colquhoun would sleep safely in his own bed, Pickett reasoned, which was more than he could say for himself. Too late, he wondered if he should have asked his former magistrate what steps he might take to forcibly evict the stranger from his residence. But no, Mr. Colquhoun had been in no condition to dispense legal advice, even if Pickett had thought to ask for it. Perhaps if he'd gone to Bow Street sooner...

But he'd been ashamed. Too ashamed to let his former colleagues know that he'd been idle since leaving Bow Street, that his plan to take on private commissions independent of that organization had proven to be an abysmal failure.

He gave a bitter little laugh. If he'd thought his situation humiliating before, only look at him now, wandering the streets of London with nowhere to go and no one to go home to. *Oh, Julia,* he thought, *wherever you are, I hope you're having better luck than I am.*

In the absence of both his wife and his mentor, he had no one else to turn to. He had always been a private person, the experiences of childhood having taught him that few people could be trusted—least of all Moll, the nominal "stepmother," who had ordered him out of the house before his father's ship, bound for Botany Bay, had even left the harbor. In fact, until Mr. Colquhoun had crossed his path (or, rather, until he had crossed Mr. Colquhoun's, having been hauled before the magistrate for theft), he could remember only one person who had commanded his respect—although that hadn't stopped the young Pickett from stealing coins from the man's desk from time to time. Still, he'd recently done what he could to atone for those old wrongs, and so now he set out across London once more, this time bound for the Butterworth Charity School.

He was still bewildered by the resurrection of Drury Lane Theatre from its own ashes, but as he reached the slums of Seven Dials, it was clear there had been no such redemption for this benighted section of Town, or for the luckless individuals who had the misfortune to live here. Unlike the deserted streets of Mayfair, there were still some signs of life here, for while the honest citizens of London slept, the city's criminal element stirred to life, like nocturnal creatures awakening from their daytime slumbers. Across the street, a trio of ragged men loitered in a doorway; Pickett took care not to invite trouble by seeming to challenge them, but kept a close watch out of the corner of his eye nonetheless. Some little distance away, a man lurched drunkenly across the dark, narrow street in answer to the summons of a blowsy woman who called down bawdy invitations from an upper-story window. Nearer at hand, another man lay motionless against the wall, either sick, unconscious, or dead; Pickett, stepping gingerly around this inanimate heap of humanity, wasn't especially eager to find out which.

Mr. Butterworth's school represented a small ray of hope in this bleak underworld, and it drew Pickett now just as it had a dozen years earlier, when he had briefly been a student there. He was not alarmed to find it dark, or its door locked; the hour was far advanced by this time, and even the most dedicated of schoolmasters would have long since sought his bed. Still, something struck him as ominous, although he could not have said what. Then the moon emerged briefly from the clouds, and he had his answer.

The words "Butterworth Charity School," once painted over the door in neat block letters, were now cracked and peeling, and a tattered paper nailed to the door announced that the building was available for lease; the curled edges and faded text suggested it had been untenanted for a considerable time.

Pickett stepped to the window, cupped his hands about his eyes, and pressed his nose to the glass. The headmaster's desk was still there, but instead of standing parallel to the wall facing the young scholars, it had been shoved aside at an angle, allowing Pickett to see that two of its drawers hung open. As for the rest of the school-room furnishings, the tables and chairs where the pupils had once sat were now tumbled haphazardly about the room. Most of the books had been pulled down from the shelves and some of their pages torn out, presumably to be burned as a free source of fuel on cold nights such as this one. A thick coat of dust shrouded everything, disturbed in places by footprints too large to belong to any youthful scholar. Clearly, it had been a very long time since any classes had been taught here.

"Looking to lease the place?"

Interrupted in his survey of the old schoolroom, Pickett turned to discover the night watchman, one of those vestiges of an earlier chapter in the history of English law enforcement, regarding him with thinly veiled suspicion.

"What? Oh—no—nothing like that. It's just—I used to go to school here." He knew his manner was unlikely to allay anyone's misgivings, but in fact, the man had taken him by surprise; the Charlies were usually content to spend their shifts tucked securely in their watchman's boxes, warming themselves on cold nights with a hot brick and a bottle of gin—although not necessarily in that order.

"Is that right?" The watchman's tone was more indicative of skepticism than curiosity. "Well, no one's gone to school here in ten years or more, and you look like your school days are long past, so mayhap you'd best be moving along."

As Pickett, at five-and-twenty, was obliged to endure a seemingly endless litany of observations about his youth, the fact that the watchman was accusing him instead of being too old was in itself enough to convince him that the entire world had been turned on its head. He hadn't the luxury of pondering this curious reversal, however, for something the man had said had aroused his curiosity.

"Ten years, you say?"

The watchman nodded, and together they left the abandoned school and walked back the way Pickett had come. "Aye, although now that I come to think on it, it's probably more like a dozen."

"Why? Did Mr. Butterworth—is he dead?" Pickett asked, thinking of his former employer, Elias Granger, now deceased.

"Lud, how should I know? He wasn't dead when the school closed, if that's what you're wanting to know."

"I see. Why did he close it, then?"

"Look about you!" The watchman waved his arm in a sweeping gesture that took in the disreputable neighborhood. "Do any of these folks look like they care much about learning to read, write, and cipher?"

One of them did, Pickett thought. He had no opportunity to point out this exception, however, for the watchman wasn't finished yet.

"No, I'm thinking poor old Mr. Butterworth was just tired of fighting a losing battle. Can't really blame him, can you?"

Pickett agreed that he could not, and after failing to ascertain from the watchman any information as to Mr. Butterworth's present whereabouts, he began to devise a plan. He had only to remain in conversation with the night watchman long enough to convince the man that he was indeed "moving along," then return and let himself into the schoolroom. He had no illusions that any of the coins Mr. Butterworth had once kept in his desk drawer would still be there—how helpful *that* would have been!—but at least he could lock himself inside and be assured of a reasonably safe place to sleep and some protection from the elements. Like Harold Bertram, Pickett was persuaded snow was in the air.

He voiced this prediction to the watchman, and the reliable topic of the weather sustained the conversation while they traversed the length of two full blocks, by which time Pickett judged it safe to part company with his unwelcome companion. He bade the night watchman a cheerful good evening and set off in another direction. Twice he looked back and saw the watchman some distance behind, although the man did not appear to be intentionally following him.

Not until Pickett looked back a third time and saw no trace of the fellow at all did he deem it safe to return to the old Butterworth Charity School, and even then he did not dare to retrace his steps, but instead turned down a side street that, if memory served, should take him back to Seven Dials. He soon had the satisfaction of discovering that his recollections of this part of London were correct: the narrow lane decanted him into one of the seven streets that were all that remained of the intersection's namesake, the column with its sundials having been dismantled and removed long before Pickett was born. Along the way, he had the felicity of discovering a short twist of fine metal wire amongst the detritus littering the street. He straightened it as much as possible and, having reached the door of the school, proceeded to put his makeshift tool to good use.

Positioning himself before the door so as to conceal the movements of his hands, he inserted the wire into the lock. He wished he might squat or kneel, as this would give him a better angle from which to do his work, but he dared make no move that would attract the attention of the vagrants still loitering about the streets. With any luck, they would assume him to be relieving himself against the wall, and allow him to satisfy the demands of Nature in privacy.

A faint *click*, more felt than heard, told him he'd accomplished his goal. With a sigh of relief, he withdrew the wire from the lock and pushed the door open.

In the same instant, a hand seized the collar of his coat. "I knew you was up to no good," growled the watchman. "Now, you'll be coming along with me. 'Used to go to school here,' my Aunt Fanny! *I* knows a thief when I sees one!"

Taken by surprise, Pickett had no time to think. Nor had he any need for conscious thought, for instincts he'd believed to be long-forgotten now reasserted themselves with a vengeance. He yanked his arms from his sleeves and ran, leaving the night watchman holding nothing but an inside-out tailcoat of Bath superfine.

"Stop! Thief!" Flinging the coat to the ground, the watchman set out in hot pursuit, swinging his wooden rattle to summon bystanders to join in the hue and cry.

Suddenly Pickett was fourteen years old again, and blind to everything but the need to escape his pursuers. He had no doubt of his ability to outrun old Charlie—the men chosen to fill the position were known for being elderly—but any bystanders would quickly realize that they stood to collect a share of the reward for his capture. And so he ran, up lane and down alley until his aching legs and heaving chest finally forced him to stop, leaning against a grimy brick wall for support as he caught his breath and surveyed his surroundings.

Just when he'd thought things couldn't possibly get any worse, they had. For now he had no family, no home, no money, no coat—and no idea where he was.

8

*In Which John Pickett Discovers
an Old Acquaintance in Dire Straits*

*B*uck up, old boy, Pickett told himself, stopping to study his surroundings as his heavy breathing and pounding heart slowly returned to normal. *It can't be as bad as all that.*

After all, there had been a time, not so very long ago, when he'd known the back alleys of London like the back of his hand. He had only to walk in any direction long enough, and he would eventually come to some landmark he recognized.

Eventually.

If he didn't walk straight into the arms of a hungry mob first.

The only question remaining was deciding which

direction to go. The fetid smell of stagnant water suggested that he wasn't far from one of the inlets formed by either nature or human hands along the banks of the Thames. If he could locate it, he could follow the river westward to more familiar parts of Town. If he could determine which direction was west. Even the direction of the river's flow wouldn't necessarily serve as a guide; if the tide was coming in, the water would flow inland, away from the sea.

"Care for some company?"

The low, feminine voice sounded a bit too refined for his present surroundings, and held a hint of the Midlands that seemed out of place here in London's slums. Pickett turned toward the speaker, and found himself confronting a slender, dark-haired young woman whose extremely low-cut gown (to say nothing of the apparent lack of any stays underneath it) left no doubt as to the sort of companionship she offered.

"Er, no, thank you." Pickett fixed his eyes firmly on her face, a pale oval in the moonlight, and was assailed with the impression that he had done this same thing with this same young woman before. On that earlier occasion, however, it had not been her exposed bosom that he had been trying not to notice, but her belly, round with child...

"*Miss Braunton?*" He stared at her in astonishment.

"How did—why—what are *you* doing here?"

"I don't know any Miss Braunton," she insisted a bit too emphatically. "I'm just Cat. Pussycat, in fact," she added, and he had no difficulty in recognizing her Christian name, Catherine, beneath the suggestive sobriquet.

She shivered, and he realized that the arms she kept wrapped around herself (a gesture which he had assumed was intended to push her... assets... into prominence) were in fact her only protection against the cold wind coming off the water. He would have offered her his own coat, but the last time he'd seen that garment, the night watchman was throwing it to the pavement, where it had no doubt been trampled underfoot by every rogue and whore in Seven Dials, unless someone had possessed the forethought to claim it to sell to one of the secondhand clothing shops in Petticoat Lane. Either way, it was lost to him. His waistcoat was the only thing he could offer.

"Here," he said, and began to unbutton it.

"*Here?*" she asked in alarm, glancing about for some less public place in which to conduct the transaction.

"No, no," he assured her hastily, belatedly realizing how she must have interpreted his apparent determination to disrobe on the spot. "I only meant—here, take this. You must be cold."

"Thank you," she said, apparently much moved by this simple gesture. She slipped her bare arms through the armholes and buttoned the garment closed over her scanty bodice, then drew her arms back inside it to take advantage of what little warmth it offered. "I had a very fine Norwich shawl, but it was stolen from me the very first week," she recalled sadly.

"Miss Braunton—yes, you may call yourself Cat if you wish, but I know it's you—what are you doing here? I thought you were to marry Martin Kenney."

She looked up at him in utter bewilderment. "The Irishman who was imprisoned for debt? What would he have to do with me?"

"You danced with him once," he reminded her. "You said you liked him."

She shook her head. "Perhaps, but that was a very long time ago."

"Only a year," Pickett protested.

"Has it really been no longer than that?" she marveled. "It seems so much longer. I was a different person then," she added, as if she were a very old woman recalling the carefree days of her youth, when he knew her to be only nineteen—hardly more than a child herself. And on that subject …

"You were going to have a child, weren't you? What happened to it?"

She was silent for such a long moment that Pickett wondered if she was going to answer at all. When she spoke at last, her voice was dull, devoid of all emotion. "I don't know. They told me it died." Her voice shook on the last word, and she added briskly, "Look here, I don't know who you are, or how you know about me, but I don't walk these streets for the sake of my health. Do you want company, or don't you?"

"All I want is a roof over my head for the night," Pickett said, thinking quickly. "If you can give me that, I'll ask nothing else from you."

"You mean it?" she asked hopefully, her dark eyes great inky pools in the moonlight.

"I'll not lay a hand on you," he promised.

She withdrew one of her hands from his waistcoat, and laid it on his arm with great formality, as if she were still a lady, accepting the escort of a suitor. "In that case, whoever you are, you just won yourself a roof over your head for the night."

He was obliged to let her lead the way, since she was the only one who knew where they were going, and although he was shocked by the discovery that she, the niece of a duke, now sold her favors on London's waterfront, he could not deny feeling a sense of relief when she did not lead him back in the direction of Seven Dials. As they walked, he put forward a few delicately worded queries, and she, finding him possessed of a sympathetic ear, allowed herself to be coaxed into divulging the sequence of events that had led to her present situation.

The tale she recounted was not a pretty one. The infant she'd borne had been the product of rape—this much Pickett already knew from his investigation of Sir Reginald Montague's murder—and her father, in spite of his best efforts, had failed to procure a husband to cover his daughter's shame. As a last resort, Lord Edwin had confronted her debaucher and insisted that he make some provision for the bastard child he'd sired. When Sir Reginald had refused, Lord Edwin had demanded satisfaction, and the two men had exchanged pistol shots at dawn on Paddington Green. Only one of the two had walked away—and that one had not been Lord Edwin Braunton.

"Could your uncle the duke have done nothing for you?" Pickett asked. "I seem to recall that he was—is— fond of you, having no daughters of his own."

"He tried," she said, choosing her words with care. "He did his best to provide me with a dowry that would tempt even the most mercenary of potential husbands. But then Papa was killed in the duel, and there was no hushing up the scandal any longer. Then, too, his second son, my cousin Freddy—we have always been particularly close, Freddy and I, and when Freddy decided it might be his duty to marry me—well, my uncle could not take such a risk, not with his elder son and heir still unmarried and childless. And you can hardly blame him for balking at the possibility of Sir Reginald Montague's bastard being third in line to inherit the dukedom."

Pickett could not view the duke's dilemma in quite so sympathetic a light. "And so he cast you off."

"He did not mean to be cruel, nor did my aunt, the duchess. In fact, she arranged for me to be taken in by a lady who provides a home for fallen women."

The last two words were spoken so bitterly that Pickett drew the obvious conclusion. "But you ran away?"

"No, I still live there. "Comprehension began to dawn, and the explanation that followed confirmed his worst suspicions. "The 'lady' turned out to be a bawd, and the 'home' she offered was nothing less than a brothel."

"Can you not write to your uncle?" Pickett asked, appalled. "Surely he would not leave you there if he knew the truth."

" 'Write,' sir? On what paper? With what ink, or what quill? If Mrs. Bleeker has such things in the house, you may be sure she keeps them well away from her 'girls.' "

"I'll tell him myself, then, tomorrow morning," Pickett promised her. "I haven't any money, but it's the least I can do, what with you putting me up for the night."

She stopped abruptly and stared up at him in dismay. "You haven't any money?"

"No," Pickett confessed. "It was—stolen." It was true, in a way. His money *had* been stolen from him, along with his wife, and his brother, and his house, and everything else he'd once held dear.

Her hand slipped from his arm, and she began to back away. "I'm very sorry, sir, but I can't—"

"I promise, I'll not lay a hand on you," Pickett reiterated frantically in a last-ditch effort to change her mind.

"It isn't that." She made a frantic shooing motion with her hands. "I wish I could help you, truly I do. But if I haven't any coins to give her in the morning, Mrs. Bleeker will— She's done so once before, you see. A few weeks after the birth, when I'd had a little time to recover—" She broke off, took a deep breath, and began again. "When I realized what was expected of me—I went out with the other girls, but instead of—of approaching men, as they did, I found a place to hide until morning. But then Mrs. Bleeker required us to turn over our—our earnings to her, and I hadn't any. When she discovered what I'd done—" A shudder shook her, one that had nothing to do with the cold night air. "I'll not endure that again, even for a man as kind as you are. I'm sorry."

"I'll still tell the duke what has happened to you," Pickett promised. He didn't ask what punishment the bawd had exacted; he wasn't at all sure he wanted to know. "Only tell me where this woman's house is located, and I'll make sure he gets you out of there."

She shook her head sadly. "And what would he do with me if you did? If he couldn't secure a husband for a niece who was debauched by a gentleman, what could he possibly find to do with one who has had carnal knowledge of half the longshoremen on the Thames?"

There was nothing he could say to that, nothing at all. There were no good options for young women who found themselves in Miss Braunton's position, but he'd thought an arranged marriage with the impoverished Irishman Martin Kenney had solved both of their immediate problems, providing her with a husband and Mr. Kenney with the funds he so desperately needed. In fact, Pickett had seen the marriage announcement in an issue of the *Morning Post* left lying about the Bow Street Public Office. It appeared that this, too, had changed.

"I'm going to your uncle in the morning, nevertheless," he insisted, wishing he could be confident that the duke would be moved to take some action on his twice-wronged niece's behalf. "There is—something else—that I must do first"—he would not allow himself to think of Julia somewhere on the streets of London, forced into the same position as this wretched young woman—"but after I've taken care of that, I will see your uncle and tell him what's happened to you."

She shook her head. "I'm sure you mean well, but I beg you will not. Let the *ton* forget the unhappy Catherine Braunton ever existed." She smiled sadly. "Perhaps it would have been better if she never had."

"You mustn't say such a thing," he protested. *And why not?* an inner voice challenged. *You did, and with far less cause.*

And then, in spite of his promises to the contrary, he not only touched her, but drew her gently into his arms and held her close. There was nothing lascivious in the gesture, and after an initial start of surprise, she relaxed into his embrace. For a long moment they stood there together, two lost souls mourning the lives they had once known.

9

In Which a Mother and Son Are Reunited

At last Miss Braunton drew back, citing the need to earn some coin to surrender to Mrs. Bleeker in the morning. Pickett was forced to let her go, although it went sorely against the grain to do so. As her slender form was swallowed up by the darkness, he recalled another young woman, one who had for several years been engaged in the same profession into which the duke's niece had been forced. Lucy might be willing to put him up, but quite aside from a vague feeling that to seek Lucy out would be tantamount to betraying Julia (he suspected his assurances not to lay a hand on Lucy would not be at all what that determined young woman would want to hear) there was the fact that Lucy lived in Seven Dials. If he went in search of her, he might well be walking back into the arms of the mob eager to turn him in for the price on his head.

No, he decided, he dared not risk it, for more reasons than one. But there was another house in St. Giles, not quite so near to the Butterworth School, where he might try his luck. And while he wasn't eager to throw himself upon the mercy of his "stepmother," he need not see her at all; he knew very well how to slip in and out of the house through one of the upper-story windows, having spent his formative years doing exactly that.

Feeling rather better for having decided on a clear course of action, he walked on, keeping an eye out for any familiar landmark by which he might gain his bearings. He eventually found one in the form of a gin house well-known to the Bow Street Foot Patrol, and from this insalubrious location he had no difficulty in making his way to the ramshackle house where he'd once lived with his father and Moll.

He did not approach the front door, but turned into a twisting, narrow alley that gave access to the rear entrance. Here he startled a scrawny feral cat, which arched its back and hissed menacingly at the trespasser.

"Good kitty," he lied reassuringly, although he made no attempt to stroke its fur, having no fancy to be scratched.

The cat blinked malevolently at him, but showed no

inclination to pursue any more active form of combat. Pickett counted doors until he came to the one he wanted, then shinnied up the nearest rainspout, which creaked ominously beneath his weight. He recalled, belatedly, that he was fully ten years older than he had been the last time he had performed this particular maneuver, and the condition of the rainspout—almost certainly the same one that had been there ten years earlier, which had been far from new even then—would not have improved in the interim. But it held firm in spite of its protests, and soon Pickett drew abreast of the window that gave into the room which had been his bedchamber.

The glass had long since been broken out and the gaping hole had been boarded up for as long as he could remember, but one of the boards (as he had discovered years earlier) could be pried up with very little difficulty. He was gratified to discover that this was still the case, although he was considerably less pleased to realize that, while a lanky thirteen-year-old boy might slip through the opening with relative ease, it was quite a different matter for a grown man of five-and-twenty to perform the same maneuver. Consequently, it took some time longer, and produced a great deal more noise, before he was decanted onto the floor of his former bedroom.

He picked himself up and dusted himself off, considering whether he should inform Moll of his presence, or if it might be wiser simply to sleep here for the night and, in the morning, slip out the way he had come, without troubling her at all.

This question was answered for him when the door flew open to reveal Moll, bearing a pewter candlestick in one hand and an iron poker in the other. The light from the candle danced over her face, revealing an expression of mingled belligerence and fear that changed before Pickett's eyes to one of surprised pleasure.

"*You?*" Her grip on the poker slackened, and it slipped out of her hand and hit the uncarpeted floor with a dull *thud*. With her free hand she patted at her improbably yellow hair, tied in rags for the night in order to coax it into curls come morning. "Well, and what on earth might *you* be doing here, I wonder?" she purred.

"I'm sorry," Pickett said, taking an instinctive step toward the window. "I hate to disturb you at so late an hour, but—"

Her face reassumed all its original hostility. Her primping ceased abruptly, and she planted her fisted hand on her hip. "And just who the hell are you?"

"Surely you must know me!" Pickett insisted. He'd feared her amorous interest in her adult "stepson" might prove awkward; now he saw the truth was likely to be a great deal worse.

"Aye, I thought I did at first, though I couldn't think

why you'd be coming to me, and in the middle of the night, what's more. But now I see it ain't so—not that I won't deny you've an uncanny look of him about you," she added, regarding him with narrowed eyes.

"Yes!" cried Pickett, seeing a hope of salvaging something from a hitherto unpromising start. "I'm Jack Pickett's son. You remember now, don't you? Your own son lives with me."

Moll cast a speculative glance at the poker lying on the floor, as if regretting she'd allowed it to escape her grasp. "My son, eh?"

"And my half-brother," Pickett said, nodding.

"Look here, I don't care how many lads you've got living with you—"

"Only the one: Kit, your son by my father, Jack Pickett."

To Pickett's utter astonishment, she began to laugh. "My son with Gentleman Jack Pickett? *My* son? What the hell would Gentleman Jack be doing with me?"

"Nothing now," Pickett acknowledged, readily conceding the point. "He's still on the other side of the world. But—"

" 'Other side of the world?' And just what's that supposed to mean?"

"As far as I know, he hasn't returned from Botany Bay."

" 'As far as you know,' is it? Then you don't know much," she informed him bluntly. "Why, I seen him in Denmark Street just yesterday."

"Denmark—?"

"Aye." Moll's scornful expression turned to one of wariness, as if she suspected that her home had been invaded by a madman. "He's still living in Denmark Street. Him and his wife."

10

In Which Another Mother and Son Are Reunited

His wife. The words spun 'round and 'round in Pickett's brain as he trudged in the direction of Denmark Street. *His wife.* If, as the apple seller's cryptic conversation seemed to suggest, he was seeing a world in which he did not exist, then it was his existence that had led, eventually, to his father's transportation. And what of his father's wife? Had his own birth prevented his father from marrying? Or was it possible that the wife in question was his own mother? If that was the case, then his birth—no, he himself!— had caused his mother to decamp.

The thought caused his steps to flag as he turned into the street where, if Moll were to be believed, his father now lived. Although by no means genteel, Denmark

Street was not as disreputable as the notorious rookery that bordered it. The seventeenth-century houses lining both sides had gradually been converted to commercial purposes, with most of its remaining residents living in rooms in the upper stories while shops and ateliers occupied the floors at street level.

Pickett walked slowly down the street, peering through the darkness for the house number Moll had indicated. He found it, and noted that here was one of the few buildings that still reflected its residential beginnings. The paint on its front door was cracked and peeling, but the front stoop had been swept clean, and curtains of cheap lace hung in the windows. In any case, it was a step up from the house where he and his father had lived with Moll. Taking a deep breath, he strode up to the front door and knocked.

To his surprise, it opened almost at once, in spite of the lateness of the hour. A woman stood there holding up a lantern, the better to see the unexpected caller. Or, perhaps, to allow the caller to see her. For the soft yellow glow illuminated a woman clad in a neat but worn dress of blue cotton, a still-attractive woman in her early forties with fine gray eyes and soft waves of brown hair lightly touched at the temples with threads of silver that gleamed in the light.

"So *there* you are," she said, smiling warmly at him.

"I've been waiting for you."

"I—I know you," he stammered, suddenly assailed by an avalanche of half-remembered impressions: a gentle hand on his forehead, a soft voice singing a lullaby or reading aloud from a book. "I thought I'd forgotten, but I know you."

"I'm glad," she said simply. "It's been a long time, Johnny."

Her speech had more in common with his wife's than with his father's, but he was so taken aback by what she said that it did not occur to him until much later to wonder at the way in which she'd said it. "You know who I am?" he asked, fighting back an unmanly urge to burst into tears.

"Of course I do! Why wouldn't I?"

He shrugged. "No one else does."

"Well, no," she conceded. "But it's a little different for me, you see."

"Because you're my—"

"Because I no longer exist, either," she said apologetically, cutting off the words he would have said. "At least, not in a form you would recognize."

He considered this qualifier. "Then you're dead," he deduced.

"Was there ever any doubt? Surely you cannot have thought I would have willingly abandoned you!"

"Moll—my stepmother, at least that's what Da called her—she said Jack Pickett lived here with his wife. He—he married you, then?"

The fine eyes twinkled with mischief. "My dear boy, do you dare to cast aspersions on your mother's honor? What sort of woman do you think I am?"

"How should I know?" he asked, spreading his hands in helpless frustration. "I always assumed I must be a—Da never told me any different. He never talked about you at all," he added apologetically.

Far from being wounded by this revelation, she lifted one delicately arched eyebrow. "While you, on the other hand, chatter like a magpie about the things you feel the most deeply."

He acknowledged this verbal hit with a self-conscious little laugh.

"In fact," she continued, taking pity on him, "we married on the fourth of April, 1783—almost a full year before your own birth. Prompt, perhaps, but quite proper. If you have any doubts, you have only to go to St. Giles-in-the-Fields and look in the church registry."

He made a mental note to do exactly that, even as he realized that he would not find his own baptism recorded there the following spring; after all, he'd never been born.

"Mum," he said, trying out the name he could not

remember speaking, "is this"—his gesture took in not just the two of them, but the street on which they stood and the wider world beyond—"is all this real?"

She considered the matter for such a long moment that he feared she would not answer. "I think," she said with great deliberation, "that it might be, under certain circumstances."

"If I don't exist," he deduced.

She inclined her head in agreement.

"But if I did exist, then you—wouldn't."

"Nonsense! No one lives on this earth, no matter how brief their stay, without leaving some trace of themselves behind. A part of me would always exist, in the person of one rather extraordinary young man. On the other hand, if one does not exist"—she shrugged—"it's as the poet said: 'No man is an island.' Every life touches other lives, and if that touch is removed, then those lives are changed, sometimes in rather unexpected ways. But I think you're beginning to understand that for yourself."

"You give me too much credit, ma'am," Pickett said with some asperity. "I don't understand any of this!"

She turned away, glancing over her shoulder into the depths of the quiet house. "I wish I could explain, but I'm afraid I haven't the time. I don't think your father ought to find you here, for he would be bound to ask questions—you are so very like him, you know—and since he'll be getting up for work soon—"

" 'Work'?" Pickett echoed, with a skeptical lift of one eyebrow that was highly reminiscent of his magistrate.

"Yes. He is underbutler for Lord Sedgewick. He might have been butler by now, were it not for his determination to spend his day off, and the evening of his half-day, beneath his own roof. Then, too, most butlers are forbidden to marry unless they happen to wed the housekeeper, and your father would not hear of my occupying such a position."

Utterly uninterested in the domestic arrangements of upper servants, Pickett gave a cynical little laugh. "I hope Lady Sedgewick remembers to lock up her silver."

"You wrong him, my dear," she scolded gently. "You don't really know him."

Pickett could not agree. "I know enough," he said darkly. "Maybe more than you do."

A board on the floor above them creaked, and she glanced uneasily upward. "I'm afraid I haven't time to debate the matter with you. You must go."

"I—I had hoped I could stay here," he confessed, and although he had not intended to beg, he could not deny that his voice held a plaintive note.

"Yes, I know you did. But there are—reasons—why

that is impossible. Take care, my dear boy." She patted his cheek, then gave him a little push and closed the door gently but firmly behind her.

To Pickett, standing alone and abandoned in the street, it seemed as if his life was unwinding in reverse, like thread uncoiled from a spool. From the elegant town house in Curzon Street where he lived with his wife, he'd gone to Bow Street and a two-room flat in Drury Lane, then to a coal merchant's house along the river, and, finally, to the narrow streets and back alleys of St. Giles. He recalled bitterly the daydreams of his childhood, when he'd imagined how different his life might have been if his mother had still been there instead of the hostile and frequently drunken Moll. Well, now he had the truth, and it appeared there was very little to choose between them. If this was the vaunted "mother's love," subject of so much sentimental verse, he thought it vastly overrated.

Still, he had no desire to be discovered there by his father—on that, at least, he and his mother were in full agreement—so he retraced his route to the river, shivering with every step. He'd lost his coat in fleeing the constable, and given his waistcoat to the unfortunate Miss Braunton, and his thin cambric shirt offered little protection against the sharp wind. Finally, having no-where else to go, he was forced to seek shelter from the elements beneath a bridge. Weary of body and battered of spirit, he collapsed onto the ground, pausing only long enough to pull a few crumpled sheets of abandoned newspaper about his ears in an approximation of a blanket before succumbing to an exhausted slumber.

11

In Which John Pickett at Last Finds His Wife
...Sort Of

Some time later—just how long, he could not have said—Pickett became aware of a slight pressure on his left foot. He scratched at it with his right, and encountered something soft and yielding—something, in fact, that felt very much like a human hand. Startled, he opened his eyes to find that it was now early morning and a fog hung over the river, through which a pale sun glinted feebly off the dirty blond hair of the urchin attempting to relieve him of his shoes.

"Here now, stop that!" Pickett exclaimed.

The young thief, realizing the jig was up, quickly took to his heels. Pickett threw off the newspapers that had made a very poor substitute for a blanket, and a headline in bold black type fairly leaped from the page:

FIELDHURST KILLER SENTENCED TO HANG

His gaze quickly scanned the column, which informed the reader that a jury of twelve good men and true
had found the Viscountess Fieldhurst, formerly Miss
Julia Runyon of Norwood Green in Somersetshire, guilty
of the murder of her husband, the eminent diplomat
Frederick Bertram, sixth Viscount Fieldhurst, and that
the murderess was to be held at Newgate Prison while
she awaited execution, at which time she would hang by
the neck until dead.

"Oh, no. Oh, nonono…"

As he cast off the broadsheet and scrambled to his
feet, it occurred to Pickett that if he'd had his way, he
would have spent the night safely beneath his parents'
roof, never even knowing that scarcely more than a mile
away, Julia was in mortal peril. He wondered fleetingly
if his mother had known about Julia, if this, more than
the need to avoid his being seen by his father, had been
the real reason she'd turned him away. One thing was
certain: he had no time to waste in returning to the house
in Denmark Street to ask.

He'd had almost no sleep in twenty-four hours, but
Pickett had never been more fully awake as he set out at

a run for the forbidding edifice that was Newgate Prison. He had more than a passing familiarity with the building, as his duties with Bow Street had occasionally taken him there. A dark, almost windowless structure designed to warn of the misery that awaited within for those who flouted the law, it even boasted chains carved over its entrances, for those oblivious to subtler allusions. More ominous still was the crew of carpenters hard at work erecting a scaffold near the main entrance. Pickett could not suppress the thought that it was intended for Julia. Deliberately averting his gaze, he hurried inside and, after interrupting the keeper's amorous tryst with one of the prison laundresses, asked to be taken to the cell where Lady Fieldhurst was being held.

The keeper displayed no surprise upon hearing this request, and his lack of curiosity was itself no surprise to Pickett; the more adventuresome *ton* bucks sometimes obtained permits from the Lord Mayor allowing them to visit the prison, where they amused themselves by viewing the miserable wretches incarcerated there as if they were animals in a menagerie. Pickett had no illusions as to being mistaken for a buck of the *ton* in his present disheveled state, but he had no doubt the murder trial of a beautiful young woman of the aristocracy would arouse a great deal of interest across a range of social classes.

" 'er cell's thataway," the keeper informed him, withdrawing his hand from his inamorata's skirt in order to point Pickett in the right direction.

"I thought the women's cells were on the other side," Pickett objected, indicating the opposite end of the building.

"Aye, but she's bein' 'eld for h'execution, ain't she?"

"Do you mean to tell me she's being housed with the men?" demanded Pickett in mounting horror.

"Keep yer skirt on," recommended the keeper. "She's in an 'oldin' cell by 'erself, there bein' no other females goin' to the gallows just at present. If you don't believe me, just ask the guard. " 'e'll show you."

Pickett thanked the man—although his thanks were drowned out by the squeals of the laundress as the keeper thrust his hand back up her skirt—and started down the corridor in the direction he had indicated. Devoid of sunlight due to the lack of windows, the passage grew darker the farther he went, and it seemed to Pickett that he could almost feel the walls closing in on him. A man paced the corridor at the far end, a man who appeared to be a guard, if one were to judge by his bored mien as well as the ring of keys he slapped rhythmically against the palm of his hand with every step.

"Excuse me," Pickett called as he approached. "I

should like to see Lady Fieldhurst, if I may."

The guard looked him up and down, but offered no comment. Instead, he stopped before one of the metal doors and slid open a narrow sheet of metal at roughly eye level, revealing a slit that allowed him to see inside the cell on the other side of the door.

"Ye've got a visitor," he informed its occupant.

Pickett could not hear her reply, but she had apparently inquired as to his identity, for the guard responded, " 'ow should I know? I'm not yer bloody butler." He thrust a key into the lock and flung the door open.

Pickett entered the small chamber and, finding the cell lit and warmed (if one could call it that) by the flickering light of a small brazier, finally beheld his wife.

She was clad in the same mourning gown of black bombazine that she'd been wearing when he'd interviewed her on the morning after her first husband's death. But now the dress was torn and dirty, and hung on her slender frame in a manner that suggested she had lost weight—an impression strengthened by the hollows in her cheeks that sharpened her chin and made her eyes appear somehow too large for her face. There was no sign of a pregnancy; had she miscarried? But no, he had never been born, so there had never been a pregnancy. Still, she was hardly the picture of blooming health: The dark circles beneath her eyes gave her a bruised look, and her golden hair was now dull and limp. Nor was it pinned up in her usual style; instead, it had been hacked off at about the level of her chin so as not to become tangled in the hangman's noose.

She was still the most beautiful thing he had ever seen.

As he stared at her, she met his gaze with one of dull resignation. "Well?" she prompted. "Who are you?"

12

In Which John Pickett Hatches a Scheme

D o you not know me, Julia?"
To be sure, no one else had, but it had never even crossed Pickett's mind that Julia might not: Julia, who had married him in the teeth of all opposition. Julia, who had professed her willingness to live under a bridge with him, if he could not be happy in her Curzon Street town house.

Julia, who now stiffened at what clearly seemed to her a shocking familiarity. "So free with my name, sir?"

"I beg your pardon—my lady." He could not fail to recognize the irony as he recalled how awkward it had once seemed, calling her by her Christian name, when now it seemed so very wrong to call her by anything else. "My name is John Pickett. I'm—" *I'm your husband,* he thought as he sketched a bow, *and we've said and done things together that would put you to the blush if I were to tell you even half of them.* "I'm—I was—with Bow Street."

"I see." Her chin came up at this declaration, but this show of bravado could not conceal the fear in her eyes. "Is it you, then, that I have to thank for my present circumstances?"

"No! That is, I'm sorry I wasn't here to—" He broke off and tried again. "My lady, I know who killed Lord Fieldhurst, and I know it wasn't you. Proving it may be difficult, but with your permission, I should like to go to Bow Street and urge the magistrate to request a stay of execution while we—while they—put together a case." Provided, of course, that Mr. Colquhoun wasn't still at home, sleeping off the effects of last night's excesses.

"I would be a fool to withhold my permission, since it appears to be my only chance of a reprieve, but you will forgive me for not holding out much hope for your success. You haven't much time to work with, you know."

"When—that is, how long—?" Pickett stammered, searching for a diplomatic way to phrase the question. Alas, there were no words that could tactfully inquire, *When do they mean to hang you?*

Julia, recognizing his dilemma, took pity on him.

"The execution is set for today at noon."

"So—so soon?" Pickett asked, feeling as if he had received a blow to the solar plexus.

"If you wish to withdraw the offer, I understand."

"No!" Far from reneging, Pickett resolved to go to Mr. Colquhoun's residence and roust the magistrate from his bed, if necessary. "I must go now—I'm sure you agree there is no time to waste—but shall I come back and tell you what I discover?"

She nodded. "That would be very kind of you, Mr. Pickett."

"In the meantime, is there anything you need? Anything else, I mean, anything I could bring you—" Granted, he had no money with which to purchase any item she might request, but in his misspent youth he had managed to eke out a living through petty thievery; he would readily do so again, if only he might dispel the shadows from her eyes.

"Thank you, but no," she said, giving him a bleak smile.

He knew her well enough to understand what she didn't say. With her execution only a few hours away, she didn't expect to live long enough to need anything beyond the contents of the small, dark cell: the narrow cot, the modicum of heat and light provided by the coals in the brazier, and the meals, such as they were, provided by the guard. He would have taken her in his arms and stroked her ravaged hair, but he knew she would see this as an insult rather than a comfort. And so he bade her goodbye, touched his hand to the brim of a hat that wasn't there, and returned once more to Bow Street.

He had all the felicity of discovering that, yes, Mr. Colquhoun was in his office, but there, it seemed, his luck ran out.

"Let me remind you," the magistrate said sternly, "that Lady Fieldhurst was found guilty of murder by a jury of her peers—"

"*Her* peers? Her husband's, more like," Pickett interpolated.

Mr. Colquhoun heaved a weary sigh. "Look here, young man, I have no doubt you sincerely think you know something, but getting a stay of execution is not as easy as you seem to think, and certainly not on no more evidence than a baseless accusation."

"It isn't baseless," Pickett insisted. "If you don't believe me, go to the Foreign Office and ask them. They'll tell you—"

But even as Pickett urged this course of action, he remembered his own failure in making anyone there listen to him, and knew such an attempt was unlikely to succeed even if he could persuade Mr. Colquhoun to pursue it. Either way, there seemed little chance of putting the question to the test, for the magistrate pressed one hand to his temple.

"Stop shouting at me," he grumbled, although Pickett had hardly raised his voice. "I've the devil of a head this morning, and I'm due back at the bench, so if you'll excuse me—"

Mr. Colquhoun heaved himself to his feet, and Pickett knew there was no help to be had from his last, best hope. He knew of no one else who possessed the influence, let alone the desire, to plead in Julia's behalf.

As he left the Bow Street Public Office, however, it occurred to him that he did, in fact, number one such person among his acquaintances. He did not particularly look forward to the prospect of begging a favor from this gentleman, of all people, and especially not in his present guise; a night spent beneath Blackfriars Bridge had, he feared, done nothing to improve his appearance. Still, the loss of such insignificant things as his pride and self-respect was surely a small price to pay in exchange for Julia's life—even if he himself could have no part in that life once it was spared. And so he trudged back to Mayfair and the Albany flat where resided one Lord Rupert Latham.

"John Pickett," he informed the goggle-eyed manservant who opened the door in answer to his knock, "of—John Pickett," he finished lamely, once more regretting the loss of the authoritative phrase "of Bow Street" that had been so useful in his dealings with such uncooperative persons as the man he had come to see. "I should like to have a word with Lord Rupert, if I may."

"Yes, er, sir," his lordship's man said warily. "If you will wait here, I shall inquire."

He departed on this errand, and returned a moment later to inform Pickett that Lord Rupert would see him— although the tone he employed made it clear that he considered this a shocking lapse in judgment on the part of his master. Nevertheless, he led Pickett to a sunny chamber where sat his nemesis, clad in a silk banyan of exotic design and addressing a plate of buttered eggs and a large sirloin of beef—from which latter emanated an aroma that made Pickett's stomach growl, forcibly reminding him that he'd had nothing to eat in almost twenty-four hours.

"Lord Rupert." Pickett tore his gaze from this sizzling slab of temptation and acknowledged his lordship with a bow.

"Farley warned me," Lord Rupert said slowly, regarding his visitor with an expression of mocking surprise on his saturnine countenance, "but I didn't believe the half of it."

Oddly enough, Pickett found this unflattering observation more than a little reassuring. The rest of the world might be turned upside down, but Lord Rupert Latham, at least, was unchanged. "You know me, then?"

"On the contrary, I am quite certain we have never met. I'm sure I would have found you, let us say, impossible to forget."

Pickett, having more urgent matters on his mind, let the insult pass. "Forgive the interruption, your lordship, but I've come to ask a favor. It—it concerns someone we both care for."

"You behold me agog with curiosity," drawled his lordship.

"It may have escaped your notice that Ju—that Lady Fieldhurst has been found guilty of the murder of her husband and sentenced to hang."

"Yes, what of it?"

"*What of it?*" Pickett echoed incredulously. "Her ladyship is innocent—as you, of all people, must know, since she was with you at the time!"

Lord Rupert's expression could have frozen water. "If you want any favor from me, you would be wise to leave my activities out of the discussion. What is it you came to ask?"

"Surely a man of your standing"—Pickett reckoned a little flattery couldn't hurt—"must have connections to whom you could apply for a stay of execution while the case is investigated further."

"The 'case,' as you call it, has already been investigated quite thoroughly by Bow Street," was Lord Rupert's unpromising reply.

"Then the investigating officer, whoever he was, didn't bother to look beyond the end of his nose!" Pickett retorted.

"I believe the man's name was Foote. Perhaps you should make your complaint to him."

And why doesn't that *surprise me?* Pickett wondered bitterly. As for making any such complaint against Foote, he couldn't, for the man was dead. Except that he wasn't.

"Damn it, man, at one time you wanted to marry her!" Pickett reminded him. "Are you really willing to let her die without lifting a finger to stop it?"

Lord Rupert's eyes narrowed in suspicion. "I don't know where you came by your information, but if we're to speak of looking beyond one's nose, I suggest you put into practice what you so vociferously preach. The fact that you, a total stranger to me, are aware that I was with her ladyship at the time of her husband's murder suggests that my connection with her is widely known. If her ladyship were to be exonerated, to whom, then, would the finger of suspicion point next?"

Pickett stared at his erstwhile rival with something akin to revulsion. "*You bastard*," he breathed. "You'd see an innocent woman, a woman you claimed to love, hanged in order to save your own neck!"

His lordship regarded Pickett with a look of hauteur that took in every detail from his lack of coat and waistcoat to his no-longer-white shirt and wrinkled breeches. "My good fellow, I regret the situation as much as you do, but—" He broke off abruptly as a new thought occurred to him. "Look here, what exactly is your interest in all this? Who are you, and what is your connection to her ladyship?"

I'm her husband. No, he'd made such a claim once before to Lord Rupert, and while it had been perfectly true so far as the law was concerned, the results had been disastrous. He would not make such a mistake again. "Her ladyship doesn't even know me," he said in a flat voice, then turned and left the house without a backward glance.

He trudged back toward the prison, his steps dragging as he pondered how to break the bad news to Julia. For there was nowhere else to turn. Lord Rupert Latham, who had once entertained hopes of marrying her, was far more concerned with saving his own skin, while the Bertrams—rather, the new Lord and Lady Fieldhurst—had clearly washed their hands of her, choosing instead to go into hiding until the scandal could be forgotten. Nor could the prison guard be applied to for help; he'd been too interested in playing slap-and-tickle with the laundress to do more than advise Pickett to "keep his skirt on," just as if he'd been an hysterical female…

An hysterical female… Pickett thought, his steps slowing to the point where those pedestrians behind him were hard-pressed to avoid running into him, whereupon they expressed their displeasure with glares and curses that were alike ignored.

An hysterical female, who might fall to her knees to beg for mercy from her captors or to make peace with her Maker and thus disguise the fact that she was taller than any female had a right to be… and who, further-more, could not really die, since she had never been born…

There was still the matter of feeling pain, he thought, recalling the throbbing head that had accompanied his accident in the piazza at Covent Garden. He did not exactly look forward to the tightening of the hangman's noose about his throat, cutting off the flow of air to his lungs, forcing his tongue past his lips and causing his eyes to bulge from their sockets, but it was better, surely, for him to suffer such a fate than for Julia to do so—Julia, who most certainly *had* been born, and who would just as certainly die without some intervention…

By the time he returned to Newgate and was once

again admitted to her cell, this plan had taken such strong possession of his brain that the prisoner, seeing the light that blazed in his eyes, was moved to exclaim, "You've done it!"

"No, I'm afraid not," he confessed, "but I have a better idea."

"No? What, then—?"

"I'm going to take your place."

13

In Which John Pickett Expounds His Proposal

She stared at him speechlessly for a long moment, then her eyes narrowed. "Who *are* you?"

You wouldn't believe me if I told you. Aloud, he merely said, "Never mind that." He glanced at the slit through which the guard might be listening, and although it was closed, he lowered his voice nonetheless. "I'm going to help you escape, and then I'm going to the scaffold in your stead."

"But—but Mr. Pickett, this is madness! Why should you do such a thing? Why, you don't even know me!"

He could have set her straight on this point, but did not. In fact, he did not answer at all for a long moment, and when he spoke again, it was haltingly. "I must do this, my lady, in order to—to right an old wrong. There was once a lady I—I cared for very much. I was the only one who could save her; in fact, I believed I *had* saved her, only—only it proved not to be the case."

"And this lady," she said thoughtfully, "was her name Julia, by any chance?"

For the first time since he'd cracked his head in Covent Garden, Pickett felt a faint flicker of hope. "It was," he said, while inwardly he pleaded, *Please know me… please say you remember.*

But no. "Mr. Pickett, I am truly humbled by your willingness to make such a sacrifice, but I cannot ask such a thing of you!"

"You didn't ask," he pointed out. "I make the gesture willingly."

She shook her head impatiently, and her cropped hair swung back and forth, caressing her sunken cheeks in a way Pickett could only dream of doing. "Even if I were to allow you to go to the gallows in my place, how could such a scheme possibly work? The guard could not fail to notice such a switch!"

"Perhaps; perhaps not. No, hear me out," he said, when she opened her mouth to argue the point. "The brazier doesn't give off much light. If the guard should open the door and see two ladies, one kneeling with her face buried in her handkerchief and the other standing over her with her face averted, attempting to console her, who is to say which is which?"

"There is the little matter of height, you know. You would be obliged to crouch all the way to the gallows!"

Pickett shrugged. "I daresay it wouldn't be the first time a woman indulged in strong hysterics on her way to such a fate. Between bouts of tears and pleas for mercy, who among her executioners would notice a little thing like bent knees?"

To his surprise, he succeeded in coaxing a little laugh out of her. " 'Strong hysterics'? Really, Mr. Pickett, you might at least let people say of me that I met my fate with a little dignity!"

"If I'm willing to die in a skirt and mobcap, you might at least agree to a few hysterics, at least until the switch is discovered."

"And what happens then? When they realize they've hanged the wrong person, I mean?"

"By that time, it'll be too late. You'll be long gone."

"But gone where? There will surely be people searching for me."

Recalling the mob at his heels only a few hours earlier, he could not deny it. "Very likely. And so you must be well away before the deed is done. As soon as the guard comes for me—for you, that is—you are to bid 'Lady Fieldhurst' a tearful farewell, bury your face in your handkerchief, and get out before he has time to get a good look at you. Go straight to Denmark Street, number seven—it's in St. Giles; do you know it? Hardly a place for a lady, but needs must when the devil drives. Ask for the mistress of the house. Tell her I sent you." His mother was familiar enough with the details of his life that she would surely not deny him this, that she would protect the woman he loved—the woman who, under different circumstances, would have been her daughter-in-law and the mother of her grandchild.

"It seems wrong, to run away and leave you to face the consequences alone," Julia protested. "If you are determined to do this, the least I can do is honor your sacrifice by remaining with you until—until the end."

"No, you mustn't," he insisted. "If you lo—" *If you love me*, he had almost said. But she did not love him. She didn't even know him. "If you linger, someone may recognize you, and then the fat *would* be in the fire! In the meantime, if there is anyone else you might send for in order to say your goodbyes, it might be helpful if the guard forgets exactly who and how many he admits to your cell over the next few hours."

She regarded him steadily for a long moment, then said, "I almost forgot: while you were gone, I was informed that the time of my execution has been pushed back. Instead of being at noon, it will be at three o'clock."

"I shall return no later than two, then." And then, although he hated making such a request of her, he asked, "Do you have any money I might use to purchase a dress and a mobcap in Petticoat Lane? I wouldn't ask, but I"—he made a gesture that took in his lack of coat, waistcoat, and anything else of value that might be pawned in exchange for ready money—"I haven't anything on me."

She lifted one corner of the dirty straw mattress and withdrew the few coins concealed there. "I can see how one would want a new gown for the occasion," she said with a pathetic attempt at humor.

"Yes, for my maid spilled tea all over my Sunday best, the silly girl," Pickett replied as she poured the little store of coins into his hand, and had his reward when she looked up at him with a swift, fleeting smile. In the absence of a coat pocket, he tucked the little stash of coins into his shoe. "I shall give you back anything I have left over. In the meantime," he added, suddenly serious, "in case I have no opportunity to tell you later, please know that when you make your escape, you will carry with you my best wishes for your future happiness."

Her eyes took on a moist sheen, and she blinked rapidly several times. "Thank you."

The words were little more than a whisper, but as he turned to go, she said quite clearly, "Oh, and Mr. Pickett—"

"Yes?" he prompted, when words apparently failed her.

She held out her hand to him, all the while looking at him as if she were trying to commit to memory the features of the man who was to be her deliverer. "I should have liked very much to have known you, Mr. Pickett."

It was almost, *almost* enough. He raised her hand to his lips. "Goodbye, my lady," he said, then turned and rapped on the door for the guard to let him out.

14

In Which Matters Come to a Head

After taking his leave of Julia, Pickett made his way to Petticoat Lane, where he scanned the stalls of secondhand clothing in search of a gown suitable for an aristocratic female. On its face, this was not the impossible quest it might have seemed, since he had learned during his investigation of Lord Fieldhurst's murder—an investigation that, in his absence, had obviously not gone well for that gentleman's widow—that ladies of Julia's class frequently bestowed their castoff clothing on their maids, to wear or to sell as they saw fit. However, when one added the further requirement that this gown must be long enough to reach the ankles of a "lady" who stood six feet three inches barefooted, the difficulty increased exponentially.

He discovered one possibility in a dark green garment which Julia—at least, the Julia he knew—would never have been caught dead in (bad choice of words, but he wouldn't let himself think of that) but which possessed the advantage of appearing rather longer than most of the other gowns on offer. He held it up to his chest experimentally, then looked down at the length of leg clearly visible beneath its hem—and looked up again to discover the proprietress and two of her female customers regarding him warily.

"It's for my sister," he said, feeling some explanation was called for. "She's very tall." Seeing they did not appear convinced, he added, "We're twins."

The proprietress merely shrugged. "It's your money, ducks."

Actually, it was Julia's money, but Pickett was not inclined to waste time in correcting this mistaken assumption. He tossed the gown over his arm and turned his attention to the selection of a mob cap. If nothing else, he reasoned, he could recount this misunderstanding to her upon his return to Newgate, and if he was lucky, he would see her smile one more time before he took her place on the scaffold...

But he would think about that later. For now, he eyed a brown checked waistcoat and a slightly worn-looking olive-green tailcoat, and wondered wistfully if there might be enough money left over for him to at least make himself presentable. *Presentable for what?* he challenged his own wayward thoughts. Even if he managed to survive the execution, it wasn't as if he could court his wife all over again. He had even less to offer her now than he'd had before. He had no money, he had no position—he didn't even have a name, for he didn't really exist.

With this lowering thought, he paid for the gown and mobcap, assured the proprietress (who still looked askance at him) that he was sure his "sister" would love it, and set out for Newgate. It was now almost noon, and while he doubted Julia would begrudge him a few pence to spend on a modest meal, his stomach roiled at the thought of eating while she sat alone in a dark, cold cell awaiting her execution. She deserved, at the very least, someone to keep vigil with her, and he resolved to fill this rôle, acknowledging at the same time his own selfish desire to spend every possible minute in her company.

As he approached the prison, he tucked the bundle of secondhand clothing under his arm and surveyed his surroundings for some alley or court in which he could put on the gown without being seen. This task was made considerably more difficult by the crowds amassing about the gallows. The size of the mob did not surprise him; the fact that it had assembled so early, fully three hours before the show was to begin, did. Unless, of course, Julia's was not the only execution to take place that day. He wondered if that might explain why her hanging had been delayed. More to the point, he wondered if it might somehow be turned to her advantage.

"Who's it for?" Pickett asked one bystander, jerking his thumb in the direction of the gibbet.

His potential informant spat on the ground, narrowly missing Pickett's shoes. "A fine lady, so they say. Killed 'er 'usband," he added significantly, drawing the flat of one hand horizontally across his throat in gruesome imitation.

"But that isn't until three o'clock," Pickett pointed out. To be sure, public hangings were a popular entertainment amongst a certain set, but surely such a crowd so early was excessive, even for a case that had generated as much attention as the Fieldhurst murder had done.

"Where'd you get such an idea as that?" the man asked, regarding Pickett with mild curiosity. "It's to take place at noon. Ought to be comin' out any minute now—here she is! No, wait, it's only the 'angman."

His face fell as the figure mounting the steps to the scaffold proved to be, not the notorious murderess, but the man charged with meting out her punishment. Unlike his fictitious counterparts on the stages of Covent Garden or Drury Lane, he wore no black hood to conceal his identity, but acknowledged with a nod several of those in the front who cheered his appearance.

Pickett did not linger to argue the point, but pushed his way through the crowd until he reached the door of the prison and stumbled inside. Ignoring the shouts of the keeper, he ran across the central hall and down the corridor that led to the cell where she was being held.

"Where is she?" he demanded of the guard. "Is she still in there? Let me in!"

With maddening slowness, the guard inserted a key in the door and pushed it open. "Won't do ye any good," he said with a philosophical shrug.

Pickett, blinking in the unaccustomed darkness, very quickly came to the same conclusion. The cell was empty of all save for a small rectangle of folded paper lying on the dirty cot. He crossed the room in three strides and picked it up.

"So you're Mr. Pickett, are ye?" the guard asked with no great urgency. "She said ye'd be comin' back. Left that for ye."

Pickett did not have to be told twice. Before the words were out of the guard's mouth, he had unfolded the paper with hands that shook, and squinted to make out the words in the dying light of the brazier.

Dear Mr. Pickett, she had written, *I am truly humbled by your sacrifice, but I must not allow you to make it. By the time you read these words, I will have departed this world for the next, where I know I will be exonerated of the crime of which I am judged to be guilty. I shall meet my fate with more courage, knowing that I had with me at the end the truest friend any person could ask for. Whatever the fate of your own Julia, I hope she knew what a treasure was hers.*

It was signed *Julia Fieldhurst.*

"If you want a place with a good view, you'd best be getting out there," the guard said. "Won't be long now."

Pickett didn't wait to ask whether the time of the execution had been changed, or to inform the man that a good view of the proceedings was the very *last* thing he wanted. The note slipped from his fingers and fluttered to the floor as he raced back down the corridor and out of the prison. The crowd had grown, if not larger, then certainly louder, shouting jeers and catcalls at the slight, pale figure who slowly mounted the steps to the scaffold. Her hands were shackled together at the wrists and held before her, so that when the guard escorting her stepped on the hem of her gown and caused her to stumble, she had no way of righting herself. The guard hauled her upright just before she landed in the arms of an eager spectator, whose neighbors offered bawdy suggestions as to what he might have done with her had her escort not intervened. The same shackles that had prevented her from breaking her fall also denied her any way of protecting herself from the rotten fruits and vegetables hurled at her by various persons in the crowd, some of whom had come armed with overripe produce for just such a purpose, while others were obliged to purchase their missiles from an apple seller who somehow contrived to move freely amongst the mob in spite of the press of humanity all around her.

An apple seller…

"You!" Pickett shouted, pushing his way through to her. He gripped her shoulder and pulled her roughly around to face him. "You told me she was in no danger!"

"I said she was in no *immediate* danger," she corrected him. "You were worried about her being out on the street without a roof over her head, and I told you she was in no immediate danger. And nor was she. Few places are more secure than a prison cell, don't you think?"

"You lied to me!" he insisted. "You knew very well what I—and now it's too late—" He glanced at the bundle of clothing he still carried, uselessly, under his arm.

"It wouldn't have worked, you know," she told him, not without sympathy.

"Very likely not. But I had to try." He looked up at

the scaffold, where Julia stood, still as a statue and just as white, while the hangman fitted the noose over her head. "I still have to try."

The apple woman shook her head. "You won't change anything. How could you? You were never born."

"I have to try," he said again, shoving the bundle of clothes at her and turning away to reach up and grip the edge of the scaffold floor with both hands.

"But why should you bother, when you know you'll fail?"

It made him angry, that, after lying to him about Julia's safety, she would delay him now with stupid questions when at any moment old Jack Ketch would give the signal and the platform would drop, Julia would fall, and the rope would tighten about her neck.

"Because if I don't do it, no one else will!" he shot back, and hoisted himself up onto the scaffold.

"Correct answer, Mr. Pickett," she murmured with a nod of approval, as a shriek went up from the crowd at the appearance of a new player upon the scene.

If Pickett heard her at all, he had no time to respond, for he had all he could handle defending himself against the guard's attempts to push him off. Having gained a foothold, he scrambled up and rose to his feet just as the toe of the man's boot connected with his chin, cracking his teeth together with enough force to make him see stars. Although he stood on the scaffold, Pickett had not yet straightened to his full height, and now he turned that inferior position to his advantage, driving his shoulder into the guard's belly and lifting the man right off his feet. He turned back to the edge of the scaffold and dumped the guard off and into the arms of some of the same men who had so crudely expressed their willingness to receive the prisoner in just such a way.

Pickett didn't wait to see if they were equally eager to bestow their attentions on the guard, for he now had the hangman to contend with. This individual had been pulling a white cloth hood over Julia's head, but upon hearing the fracas behind him, he abandoned the job half-finished and rushed to the aid of the vanquished guard.

Although the executioner's job no longer required the brawn of the axe-wielding headsman of days past, his contemporary counterpart proved himself more than equal to the task, pummeling Pickett about first the belly and then the head, driving him back until the only escape from the onslaught was the edge of the scaffold and the mob below. Their enthusiastic shouts of encouragement informed Pickett that, if he were to jump, he would find a sympathetic welcome. Still, it was an action he refused to take; his withdrawal would leave Julia alone with the hangman, who would no doubt pick up his interrupted task exactly where he had left off.

And then, just when it appeared that Pickett would be forced off the scaffold will he or nill he, a pair of slender black-clad arms, hands shackled together at the wrists, looped themselves over the hangman's head and jerked back, digging the chain links into the fleshy part of his neck. The executioner uttered a strangled cry and began clawing frantically at the garotte about his throat.

"*My lady?*" Pickett panted, staring in stunned disbelief at this hitherto unsuspected penchant for violence on the part of his gentle bride.

"Run, Mr. Pickett!" she urged. "I don't know how long I can hold him!" Even as she spoke, his attacker fell to his knees, red-faced and gurgling.

Pickett showed no sign of having heard her entreaties, much less obeying them. "I think—I think you'd better let him go now."

She did, and the hangman lurched over onto his side, hitting the floor of the scaffold with a hollow *thunk*.

Pickett didn't know how long the man would remain unconscious, and didn't wait to find out. "You've got to get away from here before he comes 'round," he said.

Already footsteps pounded on the stairs, and he knew it wouldn't be long before reinforcements were upon them. He grabbed Julia's arm and pulled her to the edge of the scaffold—not in the same spot where he had dispatched the guard, but to an adjacent side, where a cluster of blowsy women cheered this unexpected turn of events, no doubt filled with admiration and envy for one who had not only rid herself of an unsatisfactory husband, but who also appeared to be about to cheat the hangman.

"But—the mob—" Julia protested, glancing down at the sea of upraised faces.

"They're on your side now," he assured her. As the boards beneath his feet trembled with the approaching menace, he picked Julia up by her arms and held her out over the void. "Remember, Denmark Street. Number seven."

"But—you—"

"I love you, Julia," he said, and dropped her neatly into the crowd.

She looked up at him as she fell, and her wide, startled gaze was the last thing he saw before a cudgel struck him on the back of the head. Everything went dark, and Pickett knew no more.

15

In Which All Is Restored

Easy, now," a voice cautioned in a pronounced Scottish brogue. "Stay back. He's coming 'round."

"Mrs. Pickett is on her way, sir," a second voice added.

"No," protested a slurred voice Pickett dimly recognized as his own. "She...won't come. Don't want...my father...t'know."

A hand patted his shoulder. "You just lie quiet, now," admonished the Scottish voice. "You've taken a nasty spill, but you'll come about."

Pickett opened his eyes, and discovered that he was no longer on the scaffold outside Newgate prison. In fact, he was no longer outside at all, but stretched out full length on the floor of the Bow Street Public Office. Mr.

Colquhoun was bending over him, his thick white hair neatly brushed, and his keen blue eyes bright and clear. Beyond the magistrate, several Bow Street Runners, as well as a couple of men from the Foot Patrol, regarded him with varying degrees of concern.

"Sir?" Pickett struggled to sit up, but the hand on his shoulder pressed him firmly back down. "What—? Where—?"

"You're back at Bow Street with a broken head," Mr. Colquhoun informed him, adding with a twinkle in his eye, "Just like old times, in fact."

"Yes, but—but what happened? Julia—did she get away?"

Mr. Colquhoun and the others exchanged wordless looks.

"Don't fret yourself over Mrs. Pickett," the magistrate chided. "She'll be here shortly, bringing the doctor with her."

"Yes, but Julia—"

"As for what happened," continued Mr. Colquhoun, ignoring the interruption, "Mr. Carson here would be the one to tell you about that, as he witnessed the whole thing."

"Damn fool drayman can't control his team," Harry Carson informed him bluntly, and for once there was no trace of the mocking humor that Pickett so deplored. "He ran you down right in the middle of the piazza."

That wasn't quite the way Pickett remembered it, but then, given the way his head felt at the moment, he probably wasn't the best man to judge. Aside from the pain in his head, however, he felt better than he had in two days—due, no doubt, to the fact that he was warm for the first time since he'd abandoned his coat to an angry watchman. He realized with some surprise that the coat must have been discovered and returned to him, for he was wearing it—and it appeared very little the worse for whatever adventures it might have experienced in the interim.

Before he could voice this interesting observation aloud, the door flew open and Julia burst into the room. But this Julia was very different from the one he had left only—when? Not today, surely, for her cropped hair had grown long enough to be dressed in her usual style. Her hollowed cheeks had filled out, but as she approached, he realized that her face was not the only thing that had filled out: Her belly was rounded with child, to the point that the skirts of her velvet pelisse would not quite meet in the front. He realized with dismay that he'd never told her she wasn't barren, never cautioned her not to succumb to Lord Rupert's advances—or anyone else's —unless he first put a ring on her finger.

"I should have warned you," he muttered thickly.

"I'm sorry—I—"

"John!" she cried, ignoring this half-formed apology. "Darling, what happened? Are you all right?"

"Easy now, Mrs. Pickett," cautioned the doctor, a tall, thin man just opening a worn leather bag. "I never knew of any man whose condition was improved by having a woman weeping all over him."

Pickett might have disputed this claim, but his attention was all for Julia. "You—you know me?" he asked, afraid to hope.

She smiled and laid a hand on the swell of her abdomen. "I believe we are a little acquainted."

It wasn't real, then, thought Pickett as comprehension began to dawn. None of it had been real. And yet, it had seemed so very...

"What day is it?" he asked, looking from Julia to Mr. Colquhoun.

"What day?" echoed Julia, bewildered. "Why, it's Thursday."

"No, no." He started to shake his head, then decided it hurt too much and stopped. "What day is it?"

"The nineteenth of October," Mr. Colquhoun said.

The very same day, then. Pickett almost turned to look at the large clock over the magistrate's bench, but remembered his sore head and thought better of it. "And—and what time?"

Mr. Colquhoun consulted the clock mounted on the wall above his bench. "A quarter to two."

Not much time at all, in fact. And yet it seemed like days since he'd first found himself in a world he didn't recognize—or, rather, that didn't recognize him—and only an hour or two since his botched attempt at rescuing Julia, who, it now appeared, had never really been in danger at all.

He struggled to wrap his brain around the abrupt change in his circumstances—no, for they had never changed in the first place—while the doctor poked and prodded, and observed jocularly that it appeared his primary duty to the growing Pickett family would be keeping its patriarch's head intact.

In fact, he remained so aloof during Dr. Gilroy's ministrations that Julia, in spite of the physician's assurances, was not at all convinced he was capable of making the long walk back to Curzon Street, and expressed her intention of procuring a hackney—a pronouncement that had three members of the Foot Patrol falling over each other in an attempt to provide this service for her.

"John, are you quite certain you're all right?" she asked when they were alone in the vehicle. "Why do you keep looking at me like that?"

"Like what?"

She gave a self-conscious little laugh. "Like you've

never seen me before in your life."

"The shoe's rather on the other foot," he muttered under his breath.

"Meaning?"

He didn't answer the question, but instead asked one of his own. "Look here, do you mind if we make a—a short detour?"

"Of course not, if you're quite certain it won't tax your strength."

Pickett reassured her on this point, then put his head out the window and gave instructions to the driver. Within minutes they were drawing up at a modest dwelling in Denmark Street.

"I'll only be a minute," he promised Julia, then exited the carriage, giving instructions over his shoulder for the driver to wait.

He stepped up to the front door of number seven, noting that the cheap lace curtains were gone, and the front stoop would have been much improved by the vigorous application of a broom. He took a deep breath and rapped on the door. It was opened a moment later by a stout woman in a stained apron and mobcap.

"Well?" she prompted impatiently when her caller showed no inclination to speak. "What d'ye want?"

"Nothing," Pickett said, backing away. "I have the wrong—I beg your pardon—so sorry—"

He returned to the hackney and gave the driver the signal to start, then swung himself inside and sat down beside Julia, pulling the carriage door closed behind him.

"What was that all about?" she asked.

"Nothing," he said again. "I knew she wouldn't be there, but—but I had to try."

" 'She'?" Julia echoed warily. There was no doubt in her mind that she possessed his whole heart, but she was well aware that there was about him a certain gallantry toward ladies in distress. She had reason to be thankful for that particular quality—in fact, it might be argued that she owed her life to it—but she was aware that an unscrupulous female might take advantage of it in order to manipulate him for her own ends.

He shook his head. "Never mind." He had not really expected to find her there. And yet... *The fourth of April, 1783,* she'd said. *If you have any doubts, you have only to go to St. Giles-in-the-Fields and look in the church registry.* He would do that someday, he decided. In the meantime, there was another lady about whose fate he had cause to wonder. "Tell me," he said thoughtfully, "do you remember a young woman named Catherine Braunton? Daughter of Lord Gerald Braunton?"

"Why, yes," Julia said in some surprise. "What about her?"

"Do you have any idea what became of her? After

the business with Sir Reginald Montague, I mean?"

In fact, Julia did not like to think of those dark days a year earlier, when John Pickett had declared his love for her and then walked out of her life, seemingly forever. But since he seemed troubled by it, she cast her mind back. "There was an announcement in the *Morning Post* of her marriage to Mr. Martin Kenney."

He let out a sigh. "That's good," he said, and the subject was dropped, leaving Julia to wonder why he had brought it up at all.

It wasn't until they entered the Curzon Street town house and Pickett looked about at the familiar surroundings that he began to put the strange incident into perspective. There was no sign of the Dowager Countess of Wakesworth or her heavy, gilded furnishings; the room was exactly as he remembered it. His life and everything in it had returned to normal, and he could finally go back to the way things were before.

No, he amended mentally, not quite the way things were before. There was one thing that needed to change.

"Perhaps you should go upstairs and lie down for a bit," Julia was saying, tucking her hand into the curve of his elbow and steering him toward the stairs just as a loud *thump* sounded from somewhere over their heads. She cast a quick glance up at the ceiling. "I'll tell Kit to play quietly for an hour or two so you can rest. Surely the investigation can wait until—"

"There isn't any investigation." He hadn't meant to state it quite so bluntly, but perhaps it was better that way.

"What did you say?" she asked, looking up at him with an unreadable expression on her face.

"There isn't any investigation," he said again. "There never has been."

"I had wondered," she said slowly, "if you were going to tell me."

Her confession astounded him. "You *knew?*"

"Really, John,"—she gave him a look that was somehow reproachful and yet very, very loving—"give me credit for having learned *something* about you in seven months of marriage."

"But—how—?"

"You've always been quite open with me about your cases, even before we were married," she reminded him. "True, you were with Bow Street then, but now that you're acting independently, I should have thought you would be *more* inclined to take me into your confidence, not less. Then, too, I wasn't aware of any callers asking for you, or any letters that might have come from a potential client. Note, if you will, that I am not so shabby an investigator myself, having learned from the best."

He chose to let this undeserved praise pass, at least

for the nonce. "And yet you said nothing!"

"There was always the chance that I was wrong, and you actually *were* pursuing an investigation. If that was the case, then I knew it must be a very delicate matter indeed, for you to be so secretive. Either way, I knew that, whatever you've been doing—"

"Killing time," he put in bitterly.

"Whatever you've been doing," she said again, putting the slightest emphasis on the words, "you would tell me about it in your own good time—and you see I was quite right. What I didn't understand—what I still don't understand—is *why*."

Why? The question was simple enough, but he struggled to answer it nonetheless. Two days ago—no, two *hours* ago—it had seemed the most important thing in the world that Julia not know what a sad excuse for a man she'd married. But now, looking back, it was hard to remember what he'd made such a fuss about.

"Sweetheart, I don't think this business is going to work," he confessed. He glanced at the small table beside the door where that day's issue of the *Times* lay, containing within its pages a carefully worded advertisement inviting those in need of "discreet private inquiries" to apply in person at number twenty-two Curzon Street and ask for Mr. Pickett.

"It hasn't been very long," she reminded him.

"Perhaps you just haven't given it enough time."

"It's been almost a month," he pointed out.

He couldn't justify the expense of continuing to run an advertisement that elicited no response. And so, the first thing Monday morning, he would set about obtaining a position—a counting-house clerk, perhaps, or a post office guard. Hardly genteel, but at least respectable. And he would do it with a smile on his face and never utter a word of complaint, for love of the lady who bore his name and would soon bear his child.

In the meantime, however, there was something else he had to do.

Epilogue

In Which a Piece of the Puzzle Falls into Place

T here it is!" As Julia bent over the church registry, the light streaming through the stained-glass window above the altar of St. Giles-in-the-Fields cast rainbow-hued reflections onto her face and hair.

Pickett, running his finger down the page of the parish register, stopped at the place she indicated. There, in slightly faded ink, was listed the marriage on 4 April, 1783, of John Pickett, servant, to Lydia Melrose, the latter written in a round schoolgirl hand.

"She must have been very young," Julia said softly, watching his face as he traced the name with the tip of his finger, as if he might conjure the shade of the woman who had borne it.

"Yes. I believe she was."

He wished he'd thought to ask her. He wished he'd thought to ask who she had been before her marriage, and how she'd met and married his father, and, finally, what had taken her from them.

No one lives on this earth, no matter how brief their stay, without leaving some trace of themselves behind...

No, he thought, remembering the words she had spoken, she had not been taken, at least not entirely. Some part of her lived on, in himself and in his child, growing unseen in the dark, secret places of Julia's womb.

"But how did you know where to look for it?" Julia asked, after they had returned the book to the rector and departed the church. "The marriage record, I mean."

He took her hand and pressed a quick kiss to the back of it before tucking it into the curve of his arm. "Just playing a hunch, I guess you could say."

He would tell her, someday, what had happened to him while to everyone else he had appeared to be lying insensible on the pavement. Someday, certainly, but not just yet. Even after twenty-four hours, it was too new, too raw, to share with anyone, even the woman he loved with every fiber of his being.

And that was another thing: Julia—the Julia of his dream, or hallucination, or whatever it was—had been passively resigned to her fate, until he—a stranger, so far as she was concerned—had come under attack, whereupon she'd become a veritable tigress in his defense. Their love for each other, or at least the seeds of it, had been there, the one constant in a world run mad.

He hailed a passing hackney and handed Julia inside, but just before he climbed into the carriage after her, his attention was caught by a woman some little distance down the street, a short, stout woman pushing a wheeled cart. He froze, unsure whether to snatch Julia out of the vehicle and chase the woman down, or climb inside and pretend he'd never seen her at all. In the split second in which he wrestled with indecision, the apple seller put her finger to her lips, gave him a wink, and disappeared into the crowd.

"Well?" prompted the hackney driver. "Where to, guv'nor?"

Pickett stared for a long moment down the street, where no trace of the woman remained, and gave his head a shake. Perhaps he would never fully understand; perhaps he didn't have to. Whatever had happened that day, it was surely no more incredible than this, his real life.

"Home," he told the driver. "Curzon Street, Number twenty-two."

Then, seizing the doorframe, he hoisted himself up onto the step and into the carriage where Julia waited.

About the Author

At the age of sixteen, Sheri Cobb South discovered Georgette Heyer, and came to the startling realization that she had been born into the wrong century. Although she probably would have been a chambermaid had she actually lived in Regency England, that didn't stop her from fantasizing about waltzing the night away in the arms of a handsome, wealthy, and titled gentleman.

Since Georgette Heyer died in 1974 and could not write any more Regencies, Ms. South came to the conclusion she would have to do it herself. In addition to the bestselling John Pickett mystery series (now an award-winning audiobook series!), she has also written several Regency romances, including the critically acclaimed *The Weaver Takes a Wife*.

A native and long-time resident of Alabama, Ms. South now lives in Loveland, Colorado.

She loves to hear from readers, and invites them to visit her website at www.shericobbsouth.com; follow her on social media through Facebook, Goodreads, Pinterest, Instagram, or Twitter; or email her at Cobbsouth@aol.com.